MAGNOLIA HOUSE

Praise For Magnolia House

"4 Stars! Excellent...Author Lyn Lawrence has done a wonderful job of capturing the mystery and magic of Louisiana and blending it beautifully into a fascinating story. *Magnolia House* gives you suspense and mystery, love and suffering and learning how to live again. It is quick reading and makes for a delightful book to wrap the day up with. This reviewer looks forward to seeing more work from Ms. Lawrence."

—Tracey Eastgate
Tracey's Book Reviews

"5 Stars...*Magnolia House* is brimming with edge of your seat suspense and romance to keep you turning the pages. The character's machinations are believable for their situations. The descriptive narrative brings the sights and sounds of *Magnolia House* deftly to life. Cindi has a lot of questions to find answers to and will she be able to come to terms about why her father left her and her mother all those years ago. Dell is quite upset over his girlfriend's death and he too is searching for answers. Both Dell and Cindi are grieving over the loss of loved ones and that instantly forms a bond between them. Ms. Lawrence has penned a terrific romantic suspense story you won't want to miss."

—Shadoe Simmons
All About Murder Reviews

"...A clever romp in mystery, love and intrigue. The small cast of characters makes the story very intimate, and one can truly get into the characters and believe in them, understanding their motivations and desires. Cindy Lynn and Dell Comeaux are two well-rounded characters, each with his or her own flaws and past heartaches. The creative way that Ms. Lawrence weaves paranormal elements and reality into a mysterious, cohesive whole, is outstanding. Several good twists and turns in the plot throughout this book definitely make this particular story a page-turner. A cannot-put-me-down type of book. And the final twist in the story is a shot in the dark. It just comes upon you silently, then hits with the intensity of a tornado. Creative, sensitive and suspenseful, this is absolutely a book to pick up. I heartily give it 4.5 out of five stars. I only wish it would have been longer."

—Carol Durfee
Scribe's World

ALSO BY LYN LAWRENCE

For The Weekend

Stone Justice

MAGNOLIA HOUSE

BY

LYN LAWRENCE

To Brenda,
You've heard,
my dear, of how
I came to write
this one!
Love you,
Lyn Lawrence

AMBER QUILL PRESS, LLC
http://www.amberquill.com

MAGNOLIA HOUSE
AN AMBER QUILL PRESS BOOK

Amber Quill Press, LLC
P.O. Box 50251
Bellevue, Washington 98015

ISBN 1-59279-986-8

Rating: R

Layout and Formatting provided by: ElementalAlchemy.com

PUBLISHED IN THE UNITED STATES OF AMERICA

Dedication

To Lester Morgan,
my husband and hero.
He first took me to the setting for
the book many years ago.

CHAPTER 1

At last, after miles of winding, narrow country roads, the headlights of the rental car picked out rough stone, straight cedar walls and overflowing flower boxes. They marked the outline of a house. Cindi knew it must be Magnolia House, her final destination after thousands of miles of headlong flight. Flight from San Francisco, then earthbound in a small car from Shreveport Airport.

The house perched on a rugged Louisiana hillside, its appearance as natural as the huge magnolia trees that sheltered and named it. It pulsed with living energy and drew all the light of the rapidly sinking sun. Cindi swung the steering wheel, following the curve of the driveway. She stopped before the closed doors of a double garage. FedEx had delivered the front door key to her in California days ago, but she had no way of opening the garage doors.

"Consuelo should have sent the remote control instead," she grumbled, her nerves tingling with fatigue. A prickly, uneasy feeling flooded her as she left the cloistered safety of the car.

The day's light continued to fail rapidly. She hadn't meant to arrive so late, it just happened. First her flight from the West Coast had been delayed in Dallas so her arrival in Shreveport was later than she'd expected. Then after landing, she impulsively rented the car and ignored every tempting motel sign she passed. Wrong turns and unfamiliar roads delayed her even more. Now on this midsummer evening, darkness was fast approaching.

"I hope the electricity is turned on," Cindi muttered half under her breath. Fumbling in her bag for the house key, the unexpected rumble of a husky male voice caught her unprepared.

"All the daylight will soon be gone. I'm glad you got here before dark," someone said. "You must be Cindi Lynn."

Turning toward the voice, sudden fear stabbed Cindi. At the sight of the young man who stood before her, her fears calmed. His casual stance reassured her. His friendly but puzzled smile sat easily on his handsome, finely chiseled features as he stared back openly.

"I'm Lucinda Lynn, sometimes known as Cindi," she acknowledged in a starchy tone. "You must have heard I'll be staying here awhile."

"That's right, but it's hard to believe you're Cindi Lynn. You look younger than I expected."

Stung and embarrassed, she replied, "Well I'm old enough to drink, old enough to gamble. Old enough for most anything else. Would you like to see my driver's license?"

Now the young man had the grace to look embarrassed. "No need for that," he mumbled. "I'm Dell Comeaux." He stuck out his hand.

Cindi took it. An electric tingle surged through her at the contact. She eyed the man. His appearance was unexpected. Disappointment filled her for she had expected to be alone at Magnolia House. She needed that. She needed a solitary place to flee her mother's house in California, a solitary place to mourn her mother's death and her father's disappearance, a solitary place to rest and recover from recent surgery on her vocal chords. But he was so attractive she found her disappointment fading.

"Hi, Mr. Comeaux. I was told I'd be alone at Magnolia House," she challenged.

"You will be. My quarters are over there." Dell gave a vague wave toward the side of the house. "Miss Flowers just didn't think to tell you I live on the premises and take care of the grounds."

"A caretaker?" Cindi started to add he looked too young for the job, but stopped herself.

"That's right. You'll find I'm right handy to have around."

Somehow that answer gave her even more reassurance. Now she could see he was older than he first appeared. Wide shoulders strained the worn fabric of his faded denim shirt. Shaggy, shoulder length hair and a virile appearance bewitched her.

"Can't we go inside? I've been waiting for years to see this place."

"Your pa built it didn't he? For Miss Flowers."

"Yes." As she met Dell's quizzical look, Cindi felt her pale skin redden. He must know about her father's illicit relationship with the owner of the house. But he couldn't know how much hurt and bewilderment that relationship had caused Cindi and her mother over the years since her father left them.

"This place is a prototype for all the other solar homes my father built." The stilted words left her mouth and the unwilling attraction she felt for Dell grew. Uncomfortable, she turned once more to the house.

From the outside, it looked to be a closed secretive sort of a place. Few windows graced this westward facing side. The front door was sheltered and opened onto a trellised porch where pink climbing roses bloomed and released their fragrance. Opposite the entry, small awning-covered windows opened from what Cindi knew from study of the blueprints to be the laundry room.

"Please, let's go in," she said. Her voice sounded weak, its waning strength depleted. She handed her key to Dell and hoped he didn't already have a duplicate in his jeans.

Dell opened the massive door and stood aside allowing her to pass through first. Finally she was inside the house of her dreams. Dell silently followed. Cindi noticed then he was barefoot and knew how he had taken her by surprise earlier. His narrow elegant feet intrigued her. As did the elegance he gave even his very casual apparel.

They entered the house from the foyer, and a marvelous vista opened before them. Ahead lay a softly lit indoor garden, separated from the rest of the house by glass walls and sliding glass doors. The skylight above it captured all the fast-fading daylight. Living plants everywhere, both inside and outside the glassed-in space, gave tropical lushness to the interior. The scent of orchids and bougainvillea perfumed the air along with the fragrance of other exotic plants Cindi could not name. Beyond the atrium, she could see a formal living area complete with grand piano and long, sumptuous couches.

"It's fabulous," she breathed. "I've never seen anything so lovely."

"It is that. Too bad it's haunted."

Cindi moved away from Dell in a daze. Bewitched by the beauty that surrounded her, sated with the flowery fragrances, she knew Dell was only playing a game by claiming the place to be haunted.

"How could anything this lovely be haunted?" she asked.

"I don't know how, but I've seen the ghosts who haunt it. You'll likely see 'em, too. You'll probably hear them first, though. That is if you stay long enough."

His last words taunted her, held a threatening ring. An involuntary shiver rippled through Cindi…

"I'm prepared to stay until Miss Flowers comes back," she asserted.

"Maybe you will. Maybe you won't."

Annoyed, Cindi glared at Dell. Her intent to stare him down and put him in his place became lost in his hooded gaze. He reached out as if to touch her, but she moved away and dropped her gaze toward the cool Italian tile beneath her feet. A beautiful inlaid sunburst design rewarded her. She studied it with feigned interest.

"See you in the morning. I'll be here before you're up, no doubt."

Cindi glanced up, but Dell was already on his way out. He didn't look back, just moved away on graceful bare feet. A tremor of longing moved through Cindi. She wanted to call him back but the heavy door clicked shut before she could say a word. The sudden sharp sound emphasized the utter stillness and emptiness he'd left behind.

Alone at last, unease filled her. Dell obviously had ready access to the house. Consuelo Flowers probably passed out keys like party favors. He could enter at any time he pleased and do anything he pleased. Cindi shivered at the thought.

A faint trill of silvery laughter came from the indoor garden. She looked toward the sound. A flicker of movement in the foliage teased her sight. The merest suggestion of some delicate feminine form accompanied by a large dark animal-like shape half-materialized before her gaze.

She blinked her eyes. The impression was gone. In annoyance she shook off her fanciful hallucinations and turned right. Right—where the ceiling suddenly opened up to the second floor balcony. She headed toward the kitchen.

At the very least, Dell could have placed her luggage in her room. At the very least he could have shown her the rooms she would be using. How did he know she was intimately familiar with the blueprints? What did he know of the hours she had spent pretending to live here with her mother and her runaway father?

She entered the kitchen, a room whose inner glass wall adjoined the atrium. Here she found a small table laid with place mats and utensils. Propped against the waiting water glass, she saw a short to-the-point note:

Supper in the icebox. Hope you like it.
—Dell

Touched by Dell's thoughtfulness, Cindi wondered again at his contradicting nature. He'd been welcoming one moment, annoying the next. Then he'd tried to scare her off. She shrugged.

Opening the refrigerator, she found Southern fried chicken along with a salad, artfully arranged on a beautiful, hand painted plate. She sat down to satisfy her hunger. Afterward, she set out to satisfy her avid curiosity about the rest of the house. She began by exploring the combination living/dining area. It was a beautiful room evidently designed with lavish entertaining in mind.

The portrait of a lovely woman in the full bloom of maturity hung over the fireplace and dominated the vicinity. Her face troubled Cindi. Raven black hair hung to the woman's shoulders. Her dark eyes held a stern and warning expression. A slight smile curved the lush mouth, making her expression both taunting and smug. This must be a painting of Consuelo Flowers. Whatever had her father found appealing about her? Cindi wondered. This woman looked cold and haughty, nothing like Cindi's childlike, fragile mother.

At the memory of Clarisse St. Germaine Lynn, tears threatened. Her mother's beautiful face shimmered unbidden in Cindi's memory. The many years she had spent protecting and caring for her mother filled her mind. Though she'd loved her mother, she'd also been held captive by her. Forced to be a stand-in for the man who had deserted them both, Cindi had often longed to break free.

Guilt came as Cindi fought back tears. She forced her attention away from the painting and quit the first floor as well. Rushing headlong up the stairs, she quickly reviewed the upper level where several bedrooms and baths accessed the open gallery. Then her fatigue and emotions overcame her.

She headed back downstairs for the only rooms still unexplored, the master suite. She knew where the rooms were. She had already inhabited them in her imagination. She was glad Consuelo Flowers had given her permission.

"Use my rooms. My rooms are the most comfortable in the house. You will need all the comfort you can get, my child," she'd said.

Cindi, worn with grief and overcome with surprise at Consuelo's call, had not objected. She had not even objected or voiced her disapproval when the woman called her "my child." Apparently this unknown woman thought she could take over Clarisse Lynn's daughter as she had already taken over Clarisse's husband.

Consuelo, truly an unknown entity, had stolen Cindi's father. Cindi had never expected to meet the woman. She had never expected to feel the least bit of charity toward her. The woman's unexpected phone call, hours after her mother's funeral service had changed all that.

The offer seemed a perfect solution giving Cindi the chance to visit the place she'd always longed to visit. And even better, she wouldn't have to put up with Consuelo who was off on a journey to South America.

"I have to go. I have to find your father," she had explained. "You will stay at Magnolia House and protect all my beautiful treasures. And when I return, we will be able to get to know each other."

"You think there is a chance you will? Find my father that is."

"I'm sure I will."

In the dazed condition of her grief, Cindi believed Consuelo. Jim Lynn had been missing and feared dead for almost two months. Consuelo's assurance gave Cindi hope he was alive. Though she was grown, she refused to believe her father had died and left her completely orphaned and alone.

Now here in the house he'd built, she felt closer to Jim Lynn than she had for years. But in that closeness, insistent questions came. Why had her father left her and her mother? Why hadn't he ever wanted Cindi to come stay with him? Why wasn't the State Department doing anything to find Jim Lynn?

She sighed in bewilderment and felt the heaviness of tears prick her eyes. Wandering about the master suite, she found ingenious energy-saving devices everywhere. Yet the furnishings of the rooms were elegant, even opulent.

Included in the suite were a sitting room, solarium and a private walled patio at the rear of the house. An enormous mirrored bedroom, a separate dressing room and a spacious sky-lit bath with a large whirlpool tub filled with water were also part of the suite.

The water in the tub seethed with impatient motion. Cindi realized it circulated constantly for conservation purposes. As myriad images of herself glinted from the many mirrors, Cindi fought to quell imagined glimpses of sexy Dell Comeaux joining her in this intimate setting.

She soon gave up and let herself enjoy her fantasies. Dell simply bewildered her. An enigma. She closed her eyes and saw him as he'd been at first glance. She saw again his careless, relaxed stance as he watched her. She saw the small, secretive smile on his face, the way his thumbs, hooked in the pockets of his worn jeans, pulled them even lower on his slim hips.

She almost felt his compelling gaze on her now. The deep response he stirred deep within her rocked through her, shaking her. Somehow she knew it promised danger.

She brushed off her fancies and continued to wander through the rooms. In the sitting room, she found glass showcases filled with rare editions of books and signed music manuscripts. Some of the more beautiful manuscripts had been framed and hung on the wall above the case. A collection of tiny, bejeweled pianos and other musical instruments filled another showcase. Cindi promised herself she would examine them more closely when not distracted by thoughts of a certain young man she'd just met.

I'm tired, too, she realized.

After opening the drapes on the glass wall that faced the atrium, she prepared for bed. The soothing sound of rushing water in the whirlpool filled her ears. The starlight visible through the garden's skylight soothed her as she fell asleep.

* * *

Soft daylight flooded through that same overhead window the next day. The light woke Cindi gently. She'd slept the whole night through. No unusual sounds had disturbed her rest. Certainty that no ghosts had walked last night in Magnolia House filled her mind. Added certainties that there really were no ghosts assured Cindi that Dell had been playing mind games with her when he mentioned them. That conclusion made her feel good, in control.

Enticing smells drifting from the kitchen led her there to find the man himself busy with breakfast preparations. He handed her a thick mug of coffee as she entered.

"Here's your coffee. Take it out on the deck. I'll bring the food in just a minute."

"Thanks," Cindi said as she accepted the steaming mug. "I had such a restful night. I'll need the caffeine to get me going." She meant her words to put Dell in his place. She wasn't to be ordered about.

Stepping out the French doors Dell indicated, she stepped into a different atmosphere from the artificially cooled air of the house. This air was warmer, moister. This air was redolent with the scent of wild flowers blooming on the rugged hillside before her.

Ancient pines pushed spired tops into the sky and added a pungent, spicy odor. Huge magnolia trees covered with blooms circled the house. Overlaying the smell of the flowers and the aromatic pine, the pervasive, lemony fragrance given by the heavy magnolia blooms filled her senses.

She turned as Dell pushed through the doors with her breakfast tray. Once again he'd used artistry in serving the food. Her wicker tray held beautiful, dark rose pottery dishes filled with a Tex-Mex omelette and everything else usually associated with breakfast.

At her first taste, she gave him an appreciative smile. "This tastes as good as it looks."

"Just trying to please, Ma'am."

"I haven't heard anyone use that word since I moved to California. And no one has ever used it in reference to me. Makes me feel older than God."

Dell dodged backward as if she'd scored a direct hit. "Seeing as you look all of sixteen, you don't need to feel like that. I was only using the courtesy we Southerners are supposed to be famous for."

"If that's Southern courtesy, here's a Southern reply. Oh fiddle dee-dee, go on with you now, sir. But wait. I guess you might call that Irish blarney instead since that's one of Scarlett O'Hara's lines."

Dell didn't answer her. She might take his words for flattery, but he meant them—every one. She looked like a teenager, innocent and enticing in her spaghetti-strapped blue knit jumper layered over a white tank top. His feelings toward her, anything but brotherly, shook him. Mr. Jim has always been like a father to me, he thought.

He kept his thoughts to himself, remaining silent. His mouth was full of dark-yellowed country eggs and crisp bacon anyway. But he hitched his chair away from hers and closer to the railing of the deck. She would see the evidence of her effect on him if he weren't careful.

Cindi, enjoying the meal as well, felt the pull of attraction, too. Clad only in ragged cut-off blue jeans and a loose tank top, Dell's nearly bare torso demanded her attention. Perched slightly ahead of her like some wild creature momentarily at rest, his back to her, at least he would not know of her interest.

"I guess you just came over and let yourself in before I woke up. What time was that anyway? I'll try to be up earlier tomorrow." Cindi's tart words were meant to rebuke Dell for his easy entrance and way about Magnolia House.

"I always fix breakfast for Miss Flowers. I like to cook. I never trespass farther than the kitchen. You'll be quite safe from me in your bedroom." Dell turned toward her as he spoke. His amused glance played over Cindi's reddening face.

"I know that," she said. How could he know exactly what she had been thinking earlier? She couldn't look at him anymore for fear their glances might meet. And his would be too knowing.

Instead she kept her entire attention on the panoramic natural beauty of the scene before her. She feared she might never be able to look Dell in the eye again.

Once she'd finished her meal, Cindi forced her tongue to form words. "I'll be glad to do kitchen duty and clean up the dishes from breakfast since you did the cooking."

"That's fine with me. I need to mow grass anyway." Dell, apparently a man of few words, left as soon as these were out of his mouth.

By now Cindi had grown used to his short speeches and abrupt departures. After the kitchen was once more tidy, she returned to the deck. The fresh, sweet country air cooled her cheeks where the heat of embarrassment and attraction still lingered. It carried floral smells of honeysuckle and roses along with the pervasive magnolia.

She descended from the deck and walked down the slope to the south of the house, moving closer to the scene that had captured her during breakfast. Here the land sloped rapidly and a teasing hint of water glinted through the trees. The rugged terrain made her put off further exploring until she'd unpacked her hiking boots.

Climbing back to the deck where she and Dell had eaten, she turned the corner and continued investigating the deck wrapped around to the east side of the house. Here she discovered a dramatic change. Here the vista was one of elegance with formal landscaping, lovely cushioned patio furniture, and on the lawn below, a kidney-shaped pool full of aquamarine water. The land sloped upward at a gentle incline, then leveled off for the pool and its nearby pool house. It provided as civilized a setting as the southern exposure offered a wild, untamed one.

In the distance on the slope above the pool, Dell moved into view on a riding lawnmower. The smell of newly cut grass wafted toward her. As she watched, Dell glanced her way, drawn by the weight of her gaze. With hesitancy, Cindi waved at him and received an answering salute. The simple casual exchange warmed her with its easy intimacy. In full retreat from Dell's piercing gaze, she stepped back into the house through elegant French doors. She found herself in the formal dining/living area near a beautiful Steinway grand. The piano's glossy polish showed the loving care it had been given, but its yellowed, ivory keys told its age. Its true pitch and full tone were released as Cindi touched them.

Emotion overcame her as she sat and began to play. Lost in her music, she hardly knew where she was or what songs poured forth from the instrument. All the technique drilled into her through her years of lessons and practice moved her hands with precision over the unfamiliar keyboard.

Ignoring her doctor's advice, she began to sing. But it was too soon. The specialist had recommended two or three weeks of rest for her throat following the surgery. With reluctance, Cindi admitted he'd been right. Her position at the university depended on her following instructions. How could she hold rehearsals for the college choir if she couldn't show them how their parts should sound? And the extra money her private voice lessons brought would be in jeopardy as well. No, if she wanted to return to teaching, she mustn't try to sing now. Or even use her voice more than necessary.

But, at least I can still play, she consoled herself. She threw all her energy into a mixture of classical, jazz and rock sounds. She played on and on for over an hour until a tap sounded on the window.

Startled from her complete absorption in the music, she raised her eyes from the keys to encounter Dell's approving stare.

She walked to the French doors.

"Yes?" She gave the word a note of challenge.

CHAPTER 2

"A car's just driven up. Some folks I've never seen before are at the front door. Do you want me to go around and get rid of them?" Dell smiled as he spoke.

Cindi smiled back, the warmth of his gaze touching her. "No need for that. I'll do it. It's probably only some of the neighbors stopping by to welcome me." She enjoyed teasing him; he was so earnest with his concern for her. She liked the way his eyes crinkled to block out the sun. His attraction for her overwhelmed her.

"You've got old-fashioned ideas about the South. People aren't so hospitable anymore. Besides there aren't any close neighbors. Maybe you should let me answer the door."

The doorbell clamored and Cindi heard it for the first time. Its strident command urged attention. She deemed Dell too full of his own importance. She would show him she had no fear.

"No, thank you, Dell. I don't imagine whoever it is will stay long. I'm sure I can handle things."

Her answer, given to put Dell in his place, served to quell her uneasiness as well. She watched as he headed back to the mower with a nonchalant wave before she headed for the door.

Squaring her shoulders, her erect posture giving courage, Cindi crossed the inlaid marble tile of the foyer with a firm step. A toy soldier from "The Nutcracker Suite," she was. The thought brought a nervous titter, but it died in her ravaged throat as she glanced through the door's peephole. She was going to need every bit of her borrowed bravado to face the man who stood there.

The sheltering, fragrant roses formed a backdrop for her father's partner, Cliff Aymond. Next to him stood a young woman in a peasant blouse and dirndl skirt. Cliff being the one person she least expected or desired to see, she shrank back. Unaware of her scrutiny, he stood there at ease, confident, awaiting entrance to Magnolia House.

She opened the door to confront the man she once thought she would marry. Memories of their brief engagement period, when she was even younger, surged in her mind. At that time, this man had managed to tear apart her emerging femininity and self-esteem. He had scarred her deeply.

In her distress, she barely glanced at his companion. All she saw was a blur of dark hair and colorful garments as the woman turned her rapt attention and gaze from Cliff toward the opened door.

"Cindi, love. Something's come up. I need to see you about some business arrangements." In a sultry, suave voice, Cliff fired his opening words as if he feared she might slam the door in his face.

They hit Cindi like heat-seeking missiles, especially the love word. She backed away in panic from the door. Surely he would not use business as a ploy to win back her trust.

Her confusion closed her healing throat and caused her to stammer as she tried to fire back. "C-Cliff, I to-t-told you we had nothing to discuss ever again. How did you know where to find me?"

"I spoke with the college registrar," Cliff said, as he looked at her with lust evident in his gaze. He and the woman stepped into the foyer.

The time since she had last seen Cliff vanished. Months ago he brought news to her and her mother in California. News that her father had disappeared somewhere in South America and was thought to be dead. News that sapped her mother's will to live, to fight the cancer already invading her body.

Stuttering still, Cindi asked, "I-Is this about Fa-Father?"

Cliff just looked at her and refused to answer directly. "Cindi, these new developments need your attention." He took her hand and tucked it under his arm. Moving into the formal living area, he maneuvered her into a chair and seated himself on the edge of another very close by. He continued to hold her nerveless hand in his own.

It had been years since their abortive engagement, but Cindi was still vulnerable to the man's charm. With no more will than a child's stuffed toy, she sat completely immobile staring into his mesmerizing eyes. She lost what small voice she could still muster and was silent as a rag doll. Cindi wondered that she had ever been vulnerable to the man's charm. Charm? He had none really; he was transparent in his repulsive over-done appeal. How had he ever taken her in?

"First, let me offer my condolences on the loss of your mother," Cliff said. "You must know I was sorry to hear of her death. I wanted to come for the funeral, but I was unable to arrange time off." The man's manner was formal, his words sounding sincere although overdone and pompous in tone.

Cindi still stared at him. *Once I thought I loved this man. Once I thought he loved me. Now that's incredible to imagine. His falseness is so apparent to me now. How could he ever have fooled me so?*

Pushing down her distrust, she squeezed mock courteous words of her own from her dry, aching throat. "Thank you for your sympathy, and your good intentions. You still haven't explained why you're really here, though."

"I came because I have news," he said.

She could not look away from him. When she was younger and less discerning, she'd found Cliff handsome and sexually appealing. With his dark, crisply curling hair and beard, this older man knowledgeable in matters of the heart, had stolen her own. As she studied him now, the power of his gleaming eyes affected her not at all.

Cindi knew his power, this man who was well able to enthrall and sway juries and judges. She now knew too well his shallow, false concern for others, which covered his greed and selfishness.

"Well, since you've tracked me down, let's hear what you've got to say. What is this news? I hope it is good." Cindi folded her arms over her chest and fought to regain her counterfeit boldness.

"Very good news, your father is alive," Cliff declared without hesitation. "Perhaps not the best of news, for he is being held as a political prisoner."

Staring at Cliff with a noncommittal interest, Cindi realized what he was saying could be true. When her father disappeared, he had been designing and building a house in Colombia for some government official there. She could never keep those official titles straight so she hadn't a clue for whom. Her hope and belief that her father was alive flared brightly.

"Senorita, he is a prisoner in my country—Colombia," the young woman broke in. "I work for your father, Senor Lynn, until he is arrested. I am his housekeeper. I am Rita Gomez. When I see you father in prison, he say I must find you. Tell you to stay here. He say I must tell you…'stay at Magnolia House'. Those are his words." Her murky dark eyes gleamed with their own persuasion as if by sheer will power she could bend Cindi's mind to believe her.

Cindi's thoughts whirled. She shook her head as if to clear the confusion there. Rubbing her eyes, she wondered if her father really knew she had come to Magnolia House. Had Consuelo been able to speak to him, to tell him? But out of the confusion in her mind, there was only one thing she needed to hear, to know.

"You mean my father is truly alive?" Her voice shook with emotion while her stomach heaved in queasy rebellion. The floor shifted beneath her feet as she slumped toward it.

"Cindi, love," Cliff was saying as her consciousness returned.

His arms were around her. His voice a caress, he used the "L" word again. For a moment, Cindi imagined she saw real concern in his eyes.

"Are you sure he's truly alive? Can we get him out of prison?" *Do you mean it Cliff when you call me love?* If so, that would be balm to her wounded psyche, for then perhaps she could wound him as he had wounded her. For a moment their gazes locked. Then hers fell to his, mobile mouth half-hidden by his beard and mustache. Beyond any reasonable thought, she feared he might kiss her. The thought nauseated her. Instead he gave a visible shudder and lowered her back into the chair.

"Yes, he is alive and we are already doing everything possible to ensure his release. Consuelo is already in Colombia—but of course you must know that. Her mega bucks should have some influence. The government there needs money plus she has family connections there as well. Some are highly placed in the government. We have a good chance he will soon be free. A very good chance."

"Yes," Cindi said. "I know Consuelo is there. Is there anything I can do?" she asked, her belief that her father was alive and well, flaring brightly.

"You need rest and quiet. The best thing you can do is stay here as your father has asked you to do. Consuelo must want you here, too. I'm going back to Shreveport to my office to work on getting Jim out. Rita can stay here with you. She's a good cook and will keep your company. I don't know why Consuelo ever thought you should stay here alone in this secluded place."

Cindi straightened her spine and lifted her chin once again. Once more, her soldier's pose gave her courage. "Consuelo knew this place is exactly what I need, a place to be alone. A quiet place to grieve, a place where my voice would have a chance to rest and heal. You may not know I've just had surgery to remove a polyp from my vocal chords."

She brushed aside Cliff's sympathetic murmurs that he hadn't known this and continued to talk. "I'll be glad for you to stay though, Rita. I know there's so much you can tell me about my father. You and Dell can work out the cooking arrangements between you."

With a look of surprise Cliff asked, "Who's Dell? He can't work here. There's never been any staff here at the house."

Cindi's uneasiness over Dell's presence returned full force. After all Cliff must be familiar with arrangements at Magnolia House, but she denied the uneasiness and answered, "Oh, he works here, but you could never call Dell 'staff.' He's much too independent for that term. And he doesn't live here in the house, just somewhere nearby. I'm not sure where."

"Must be some stray Consuelo found," Cliff said.

Cindi found the statement offensive. "Dell says he's the caretaker, but he also likes to cook. He's fixed me some terrific meals."

"I'll have to meet him," Cliff said in an oddly menacing tone. "Just remember. Your father is alive. And we're going to get him home safe. I'll see you in a few days."

* * *

Cindi moved restlessly on her bed. A sharp sound penetrated the strands of slumber that claimed her. "Father, father," she murmured in her sleep, using her father's name as a mantra to invoke safety.

Silence fell in the room for a few moments. Then the strains of Debussy's *Claire de Lune* crept faintly in from the piano and lured her from sleep. Her bedside clock read midnight as Cindi glanced at it. She raised her head from the pillow and glimpsed a shadowy figure standing near the piano. The drapes on the glass-walled bedroom weren't open enough to allow more than a teasing hint of the person coaxing the music forth.

Curiosity, not fear, was Cindi's first response. She reached for her robe, but the movement must have been seen by the pianist. With an abrupt chord, the music stopped and the figure vanished. Cindi blinked and rubbed at her eyes. When she opened them, she saw only an empty room filled with the moonlight so beautifully celebrated by the music seconds ago. There was enough silvery light for her to see there was no one near the instrument.

"If I'm supposed to be seeing after the place, I guess I'd better find out what's going on," Cindi muttered as fear seized her now. Tremors and spasms twitched in her legs, but she compelled herself to ease toward the living room to seek the intruder. The glass door of her bedroom responded to her tugs with a sighing hiss of sound as it slid open at last.

Passing through the hall between the bedroom and atrium, Cindi thought she saw a fleeting glimpse of a slight form in the verdant greenery of the indoor garden.

"Enough is enough," Cindi exclaimed a little louder, hoping the interloper would think she spoke to a companion. "Where are those lights?"

Fumbling along the wall for the switch, she remembered the master panel in the foyer. As she touched it, illumination for the atrium, living and dining areas and hall all came on at once. Light bathed every bit of the area with no shadows left behind. With brilliance to spare, Cindi walked fearlessly into the living room and straight to the piano. Something glimmered there.

"Someone has been in my room," she breathed as she picked up one of the jewel encrusted piano miniatures. She studied the elegant trinket with dismay.

Then a crimson spot shining on the keyboard drew her attention. There on the lovely, yellowed keys, she saw a sticky viscous substance that adhered to her finger as she touched it. Raising her hand, the salty rich smell of blood filled her nostrils. Roaring filled her head.

What was going on here? Who was here in the house? Cindi's overwrought senses rebelled and a ragged scream tore from her healing throat bringing sharp pain with its passage.

"Senorita? Senorita Cindi? What is wrong?"

Rita's piercing voice drew Cindi out of the haze of terror that enveloped her. "Oh, Rita. I'm so glad you're here."

"I hear you scream like the devil himself chase you with his pitchfork. What happens?"

"Didn't you hear the music? Didn't it wake you?"

"I hear nothin' but you scream. What music is this? Come, let us go to your room. Tell me about this music you hear."

As her terror faded, Cindi noticed Rita for the first time. The other woman wore a slinky, black satin nightgown that barely contained her voluptuous bosom and generously revealed her other curves. A filmy peignoir had been thrown over the gown. Rita's long dark hair, which Cindi had only seen braided and formed into a coronet, now hung loose and flowing to her waist and beyond.

Like some film director's idea of a call girl and her smell matched her appearance. "Uh-huh-huh, uh-huh-huh." Cindi coughed to strangle the hysterical laughter bubbling up and threatening to further damage her throat.

"Your throat is hurting. Lie still and I will fix something to soothe it, senorita. You will tell me all about the music when I return."

Rita left for the kitchen and Cindi remembered the small, misplaced piano. She retrieved it and went to put it in its rightful place among Consuelo's treasures. Rita came into the master suite as she was doing so.

"This was on the piano," she told Rita as she took the steaming cup of hot chocolate from the maid. The woman's eyes gleamed at the sight of the costly trinket.

"This music you hear, it is, how you say, a classical piece?"

"Yes," Cindi agreed. "Do you know much about classical music?"

"I do not, senorita. Whom do you think was playing?"

"That's something I do not—don't know either," Cindi responded, then grinned and chuckled. "Dell claims this place is haunted. I guess this must be that ghost he talked about. He said I would hear her before I ever saw her."

"A ghost? And I miss it all. I hear nothing. Maybe you just dream it," Rita ventured. She appeared unconvinced of the presence of any supernatural beings and kept on talking in a calming manner. "Let me stay awhile and sit beside your bed until you fall asleep." Cindi welcomed the other young woman's brusque, no-nonsense manner, but she couldn't believe she'd dreamed any of the night's strange happenings. She was sure she had heard someone playing the piano. What puzzled her was why it had taken her scream to waken Rita.

"Please stay," she said, even as she noticed Rita's avaricious glances roaming the room. Greed gleamed from the woman's dark eyes as well. Did she offer her presence to comfort and soothe, or to better assess the many treasures in the rooms? Cindi's curiosity and need for company overcame her suspicions. "Tell me about my father? Tell me about your country," she said.

"I will do that," Rita replied. "Your father is wonderful man. Your father love my country. I will tell you of it. It is such a place. Emeralds, gold and platinum are in her mines. Jaguars, parrots and even '*el tigre*' in her jungles. Coffee, and yes, it is true, marijuana and coca are in her fields. Such a place."

"What is this el tigre you speak of?"

"Is jaguar who can change into woman and back again."

Cindi laughed. "That's impossible."

"Yes, senorita," Rita agreed in a soothing voice with a hint of mirth. "Let me talk of more pleasant things."

Rita stayed near the bed in a comfortable rocker and talked of Colombia until Cindi was drowsy. The only jarring note was Rita's assertive scent, which seemed so oddly familiar to Cindi. Still she listened gratefully to Rita's fabulous tales of her homeland, where, according to the domestic, emeralds were still to be found in abundance, and gold and platinum mines lined the streets. Cindi knew such tales were make-believe, but she listened hoping for some additional mention of her father. Eventually she sank back into sleep, but even then her mind struggled to remember the name of Rita's scent. She was sure she knew the name of the robust fragrance.

CHAPTER 3

Early morning sun poured through the windows of Dell's small quarters on the far side of the swimming pool. The light woke him. He groaned, jumped up, straightened his futon, and started his day. The pool house where he lived was divided into a changing area for swimmers as well as a completely separate space where his own living quarters were. He liked the small, cluttered room he was allotted. It suited him just fine.

The room held a minuscule kitchenette and, behind a partition, a minimal bathroom. It was all he needed. If he really wanted to cook, the kitchen at the main house was at his disposal as well.

Dell kept the biggest section of his room filled with piles of papers and books placed conveniently near his favorite places to sit. Mounds of discarded clothing lay where he'd shucked them as well. Finished and half-finished paintings hung on every inch of available wall space and more were stacked against the walls. Sketchbooks crowded one small table.

The half-done painting on his easel drew Dell's critical attention. His mentor, Jim Lynn, had commissioned this portrait before leaving for Colombia months ago. While he searched Cindi's pictured face, Dell idly moved his fingers over the strings of his guitar. Totally frustrated, he leaned down and rested the instrument against the easel's tripod legs. He started daubing paint on the picture, then paused.

For a model he'd been using a photograph of Cindi at age twelve. This was her age when her father left home. Dell studied Cindi's sad little-girl countenance and remembered the many times Mr. Jim had talked of how he hated leaving her behind.

Mr. Jim had known that her mother, a staunch Catholic who abhorred divorce, would never allow Cindi to visit him. After all, he was living in open sin with another woman. Without a divorce decree, no court order existed to allow him visitation. He'd asked Dell to do the painting in an effort to recapture the little girl he remembered and loved and missed.

That's why I didn't expect the grown-up Cindi to look so different, Dell thought. Cross-legged on the floor in the sun, he began to scribble in the book he used to record his thoughts. He wrote about Cindi's arrival. As he wrote, he tried to untangle his conflicting feelings for her. The beautiful young woman who arrived at dusk two days before did not fit the image that had been in his mind until then.

He began his entry with these words—

"Miss Lucinda Lynn got here just about dusk the other day. I never knew her name was Lucinda. That's way too starchy for her. Cindi fits her much better.

"I never knew she would look so grown-up or so beautiful. When she opened her car door and got out, her body was outlined against the sunset sky. She's spectacular. Awesome.

"She stretched, natural as a cat to get out the traveling kinks. Why not? She didn't know I was watching. Miss Flowers hadn't even told her I was here so she acted a lot surprised and a little scared when I walked up behind her.

"Her long, pale hair backlit by the fading sunlight, haloed her face. Her hair is so beautiful—looks soft as a baby kitten. I'd love to touch it to see if it is. I thought its color was strawberry blonde until we got into the house. Then I could see it's the same shade as Mr. Jim's—platinum blonde.

"She wore it loose almost down to her waist. The front part was pulled back and braided in a single plait. But wisps had worked out of the braid and feathered around her face. I ached from wanting to smooth those wisps back.

"I waited for just the right moment to let her know I was around. Then I couldn't say much because when I first looked full in her face, I drowned in her eyes, blue as the bluebonnets of our neighbor state to the west. All the air left my body and my brain turned to mush.

"I just stood there like some dumb, speechless dope. Looking at her, all I knew was that more than anything I wanted to paint her just as she

is now."

Dell went on, filling page after page with the details of Cindi's sensitive face that revealed every thought that passed through her head. He added details his artist's eye had seen, the color of the cream shirt she had worn with the pale blue linen slacks. The narrow navy belt that had cinched her tiny waist. He felt guilt at the longings stirred by his memories. He'd always thought of Cindi as his sister.

Dell duly recorded Cliff Aymond's visit and told of the arrival of the Colombian woman, Rita Gomez. He described the "dagger stares" Rita aimed at Cindi anytime she thought no one might notice.

"The Colombian woman must be jealous of Cindi."

After that last sentence, Dell snapped the small book closed. Tossing it onto the nearest pile, he stretched and lengthened his wiry, lithe body into a straight, smooth line.

Stepping out onto his small brick patio on the side away from the main house, Dell faced the morning sun. There with controlled grace, he began his morning exercises. That was how Cindi found him.

She was struck motionless and dumb by the agile, masculine beauty of his half-clothed body. Today, his trunk was completely bare save for brief ragged blue jean shorts. They hung below his taut waistline, exposing his deeply tanned, muscled torso. His movements were so open and revealing, she felt she was seeing something private and forbidden to public view.

Unable to move or look away, she watched as Dell moved his narrow, sensitive hands in an intricate pattern of slicing blows and jabs. At the same time, his long, muscular legs moved in powerful kicks and jabs, carrying him over the level space with lightning speed. He whirled and returned using the same movements, his long hair streaming as he turned.

Though he must have been aware of her presence, he didn't acknowledge it, but continued with the set pattern of his moves. They were arresting, yet oddly calming. The rhythm with which he moved approximated a silent music. As graceful as a dancer, his face showed stern concentration and control.

He finished with an abrupt backward flip, his one graceless move. Propelling himself solely by the power of his legs and abdominal muscles, up and over he revolved, landing upright almost on top of her.

Plop! The sound of his bare feet slapping the bricks moved Cindi at last. As she jumped away, shock forced harsh words from her sore throat. The words came even as the beauty she'd just viewed constrained her to remain silent.

"Was all that for me? You must enjoy showing off—maybe you're trying to scare me off instead." She was sure somehow that final move was not always a part of his exercises.

"No, ma'am, this is the same stuff I do every morning. They're kung fu movements I have to practice. Besides, why would I want to scare you off? You need to stay. You give the whole place class."

Cindi shrugged and laughed. "I'm not sure why I've got this feeling you want me out of here. Like maybe, you want the place to yourself. You have to admit you haven't made Magnolia House sound very inviting with all your talk of spooks and ghosts."

"I'm sorry if I've made you uneasy or unwelcome. I really didn't mean to. Let me show you how great the place really is. How about going on a hike in the woods with me today? Your pa always liked that. Would a nice saunter through the woods make up for my lack of manners so far?"

Cindi couldn't take her gaze off his strong, beautifully shaped lips. This was the longest speech she'd ever heard from him. She stalled for time to find her answer for his invitation. Instead all she could think of was how incredible it was that he wasn't even out of breath after his exertions. The only sign of his recent, brisk movements was a light sheen of sweat filming his taut muscles.

"I guess we could go hiking," she finally said. "I've been wanting to explore the area." She fidgeted and moved away from him. How could she walk with him in the woods when his very presence filled her with tingling chills and hot-and-cold flushes? She hoped the path would be wide and easy so he wouldn't need to give her a helping hand. Lord knows how that would make her feel.

But the desire to wander where her father had, overcame her caution over being alone with Dell.

The news she'd come to give him of last night's frightening midnight concert somehow seemed unimportant now. It might please him to learn of her fright. After all, he'd been the one to insist the house was haunted. No, she decided, now was not the time to tell him.

"I'll help Rita rustle up a picnic lunch. We can make the hike an all-day expedition," Dell coaxed, in a deep, compelling voice. "You go on back to the house and start getting ready. Put on good walking shoes and jeans. Tai and I will come find you soon."

Cindi shot him a questioning look.

"Tai—he's my dog. His whole name is Tai Chen but I call him Tai for short."

As his name was repeated, the hound raised his huge head and got stiffly to his feet. Wrinkles of excess skin covered the animal's body. His lugubrious face was so droopy. Cindi gave a laugh of delight.

At that musical sound, the dog's entire hindquarters began to move as his curly, stumpy tail furiously waggled back and forth. He moved toward her, his rear continuing to thrash in furious movement. Cindi bent to fondle his small droopy ears, scratching the folds behind them gently. Tai's mouth stretched into a grin of purest pleasure.

"What a wonderful dog! If he's going, I'm definitely up for this hike. I've never seen a dog like him before."

"Tai's my Chinese lion dog. Well, not really. I think that's actually the Pekinese. Tai's breed is known as Shar-pei, but I call him a lion dog because of his huge shoulders. It's not a breed commonly found around here."

"There's nothing common about Tai," Cindi retorted as she turned to stroll back to the main house. With a flip of her hand for good-bye, she retreated to get ready for the hike. As she left, she reasoned there was nothing commonplace about Tai's master either. But he'd never know she thought that.

Dell kept a restraining hand on Tai's collar to prevent him from trotting off after Cindi. The dog seemed mightily taken with the beautiful new occupant of Magnolia House. He seemed ready to follow her anywhere.

* * *

"Be careful where you step. More than likely, snakes will be out sunning today," Dell cautioned as they started down the narrow path through the woods.

Cindi's enjoyment of the flowers blooming on every side faded at his words. So the woods were filled with hazards as well as beauty. The early summer sunshine that warmed them might lure the snakes out as well. So what! She shrugged off the fears Dell's words conjured. Her heavy hiking boots with her jeans tucked into the tops would protect her.

In her fragile voice, she chided Dell, "You're trying scare tactics again. You'll find I don't scare all that easily." She dismissed his warning, though she noticed he wasn't barefoot for their hike. Instead he wore sensible heavy boots like hers.

"I wish you'd realize that far from trying to scare you away, I'm really trying to convince you to stay forever."

Cindi rolled her eyes in wonder over that remark. She took a deep breath to regain her poise. The lung full she got was filled with fragrance from the flowering trees and wild flowers. It was redolent with the spicy tang of the pines as well and soothing to her healing throat. She expelled the breath and let the distress over her mother's lingering last days of suffering drop from her.

Consuelo had been right. This change of scenery was just what she needed. Then she smelt the underlying fetid odor of mud and decay. A typical Louisiana odor, it brought her younger days in the state back to her with a rush of bittersweet memories.

"Is there a swamp near here?" she asked as she tried to push those memories away.

"No. You must be smelling the boggy mud on the banks of Loggy Branch."

Cindi heard it then. A musical ripple coming from moving water. "Loggy Branch? Oh that must be the stream I caught sight of from the deck. Why do you call it a branch?"

"I don't know. That's just what folks call it around here. Probably in other parts of the country—like California—people might call it Loggy Creek instead."

Cindi let one short chuckle escape. The stream came into full view then and began to follow the trail, its smell and sound adding vitality to the atmosphere. Soon stepping stones formed a crossing over the water. Dell motioned; they would take it. As they moved from stone to stone, Dell gave Cindi his hand for balance. As their hands came together, she felt electricity tingle through her. She tried to pull away and almost over-balanced them both.

Dell betrayed his own reaction to the touch and dropped her hand as soon as they had safely negotiated the stream. His abrupt withdrawal gave Cindi mixed emotions. First came the irrational fear that her touch was repellent to him. Then she knew an intense longing to feel his hand in hers again swept over her.

"When we get over the fence, we'll be off of Miss Flowers' land," Dell said as they climbed a stile over a barbed wire fence. "This fence is her boundary line."

As they rested, seated side by side on top of the stile, Cindi decided to share the memories stirred by their hike. "We lived in Lake Charles in South Louisiana when my father left us to come here to live with Miss Flowers," she began. "Lake Charles is in the far southwestern corner of the state. And Magnolia House is up here in the far northwestern corner of the state. I used to believe he did it on purpose—to get as far away from us as possible."

"You were such a little girl, you probably thought he left because of something *you* did," Dell said softly.

Cindi nodded. "I did. It was quite some time before I realized he came here because of Miss Flowers. I was glad it wasn't my fault." *And then I resented my mother because she wouldn't let me see him.*

"Mr. Jim is really a good man, Cindi. I hope you don't still hold that against him."

"No, since I've grown up, I now know that when a person thinks they love someone, they will do anything to be with that person."

"Your father does love you, Cindi. And I think he never really quit needing to see you," Dell said. Cindi and Rita had both told him the purpose of Cliff's visit. Now he added his hopes that his mentor would soon be home. "When Mr. Jim comes home, I hope you will tell him you forgive him."

"I have forgiven him and I hope I get that chance." Cindi stopped, then went on with her memories. "Mama and I stayed in Lake Charles until I graduated from high school, then Grandmother St. Germaine became ill and we went to live with her in California. She needed us."

"Don't ever forget that your father may not have needed your mother, but he always missed and needed to see you."

Cindi shrugged. "Maybe I will get to see him soon."

Dell made no further response. Cindi sighed and let her memories fall behind her. Tai had been exploring on his own. Now he returned to look at them as if wondering why they weren't roaming and romping about with him.

"Come on," Dell urged. "Tai's wondering why we're so lazy. There's this old church I want you to see. It's called St. Elisabeth Baptist Church. It's been here since 1890, and it's still in use. Once a month there's a worship service and funerals and weddings sometimes."

"Sounds interesting. Let's go."

"Since you're too far away to visit your mother's grave, I thought you might find comfort walking through this old cemetery."

Dell's understanding touched Cindi. Wandering through the old tombstones, she stopped to read some of them. There were many old "resting places" as Dell called them, but among them was one so raw and new it was as yet unclothed by grass. Tai gave an agitated, soft woof, and shook himself vigorously as they passed.

"That's Lonnie Benson's grave. He passed away just a few days ago. You can see all the rest of his family is buried here. He was the last of his line." Dell's voice was quiet and respectful.

On the temporary cardboard marker, Cindi noted the date of the man's death. Only two days after her mother's. She breathed a silent prayer for her mother's soul as well as that of Lonnie Benson. Dell had moved away as she stood there.

She found him standing before a marker that read "Cordelia Carver... Born November l, 1980... Left this life October 31, 1997." She moved to stand beside him, and saw a tear gleaming at the corner of his eye.

Cordelia, what a romantic name. Who was she? Why were there traces of tears on Dell's cheek? Questions crowded Cindi's mind, but her sore, tender throat and Dell's own silence held her words at bay. "Let's find a place to spread our food," Dell said, turning toward the small frame church.

After circling the building for a suitable spot, they ended up using a rough table built between two trees. It was used Dell explained at "dinner on the ground" time.

That term puzzled Cindi, but once again she kept silent. She was sure in time she would find out exactly what "dinner on the ground" meant. And maybe who Cordelia Carver might be. And what Cordelia meant to Dell. The whole place was held in a quiet thrall far removed from Cindi's frenetic life on the West Coast. She gathered the peacefulness around her like a mantle and felt it calm her sorrow and ease her pain. She refused to disturb her newfound serenity by such trivial concerns.

Dell pulled a soft, worn quilt from his knapsack and spread it over the ground. "Let's rest awhile," he invited as he stretched out.

In the warm midday hush, when even the birds' singing sounded drowsy and muted, Cindi followed Dell's lead. "This is nice," she said as she lay on her side, supporting her shoulders and head with one arm.

Dell lay flat on his back and scanned the sky. "I like to look at the clouds and see what shapes I can find. Look. There's a unicorn. No, wait, it's turning into an elephant," he drawled. "Maybe it's really a lion dog like Tai."

"That's nice," Cindi murmured again in a noncommittal, drowsy voice as she let her thoughts wander. She thrust them far from the man who lay an arm's breath away.

This was the countryside her father had known. These were the woods he had wandered in. The simple beauty and peace of the place enticed her. Surely the quietness of Miss Flowers' home and its surroundings had been part of the woman's undeniable appeal for her father.

She knew his life with her mother had never been peaceful or serene. Too many times she had heard them arguing. Her mother seemed to have always been crying and upset. Until the day had come when she overheard them in the kitchen.

She'd stood on the small, enclosed stairs that led from the second floor directly to the kitchen. Entirely hidden from sight of her parents, she'd been completely vulnerable to their angry words to each other. That was the day her father left for good. She could still hear her mother begging him not to go. That was the day Cindi vowed no man would ever have the power to make her beg some man as she had heard her mother do.

The back door slammed behind her father as he left. Her mother's moaning sobs had drawn Cindi down the staircase and into the kitchen to comfort her. But all the while in her childish mind, she had longed for someone to comfort her instead.

Now a warm, moist tongue on her cheek drew her back to the noonday warmth of the present. The dog had returned from his investigations and found a spot on the quilt right between Cindi and Dell. His "hello" lick to Cindi's face was accompanied by an attempt to wag his almost nonexistent tail.

Heat poured from Tai's body and a doggy smell rose from his scanty fur. Neither his damp greeting nor his odor bothered Cindi. She welcomed the diversion of his company and the comfort of his presence.

"Hello, yourself, Tai," Cindi said as the dog continued to apply his tongue to her face. Absently she rubbed the dog's large head in pleasure. Tai panted noisily and sent fawning looks of gratitude at her as she petted him.

"Tai's taken to you."

Dell's words drew Cindi's glance to him. Their eyes met in an endless gaze. His measuring look pulled at her until she knew herself to be hopelessly mired in the depths of his hazel eyes. In their yellow-green pools, she saw herself reflected.

"Dell," she croaked, but he raised one hand to shush her.

He took her free hand with his and traced the veins on the back of it with his thumb. His touch left trails of heat behind. He raised her hand to his lips and pressed a courtly kiss there. Then he pulled her to her feet. They stood inches apart, joined nowhere except their two hands which remained entwined. His moved over hers, rubbing her palm with his thumb in a circular, soothing manner.

"Let's see if the church is open," he said.

With a long, ragged breath, Cindi allowed herself to follow Dell toward the church. "Why?" She asked.

"The bottom's about to drop out and we are going to get soaked if we don't take shelter."

His words, nonsense to her at first, made perfect sense when Cindi looked up and noticed for the first time the overcast sky. The white, towering thunderheads Dell had named were now massed together, an ominous gray in color.

The first, fat drops of rain fell as she and Dell raced to fold up the quilt and gather all the picnic remains. Laughing at their haste, they sped to the haven of the small building. As they entered the quiet, oppressively warm space, a booming crash of thunder rang through the air, shaking the building with its power.

"That was close," Cindi gasped as her startled movement brought her up against Dell who circled her protectively with his arms. Emotions rose in a tumult within her.

"I thought you didn't scare easily," Dell said. "Looks like it just takes a loud noise to get you just where I want you."

There was hesitancy in their embrace for all Dell's teasing words. Cindi wondered at the comfort she found in this near stranger's arms.

Dell drew her down beside him on the last pew. He stroked her hair with compulsive moves like ones used to soothe a fretful child.

"The storm will soon be over. We're safe here," he murmured.

Cindi relaxed, her jumpy nerves quieted. Aware of the reality of his nearness, she sensed peace in the sanctity of the small church. It was plain and bare, unlike the churches where she usually worshiped.

The dry smell of old hymnals and the sharper scent of ozone released by the bursts of lightning were all part of the calm she felt. The absence of saints' statues and votive candles didn't keep her from finding comfort. She drifted near sleep.

The feel of Dell's lips on her shoulders and neck and finally on her own lips could have been only a dream. As his sensitive, mobile mouth claimed hers in a sweet phantom caress, her eyes flew open. Immediately Dell stood up and moved away from her.

"I believe the storm's over for today. Let's start for home," he said.

Tai roused from his place at their feet. With his stiff-legged gait, he headed for the door.

The little group made their way back through the soggy churchyard. This time, instead of going through the woods, they walked along the gravel road, a longer, drier way back to Magnolia House. Still it wasn't dry enough for Tai, who hated the dampness of the ground. The dog raised each foot as high as possible with every step. Fastidiously, he shook his paws over and over.

"Your pa means a lot to me, Cindi," Dell said as they walked along. "He seems like my own pa sometimes. I guess we'll both be glad when he comes home."

"Maybe it won't be long."

"Your pa helped me. He's my mentor. When I got suspended from the art department at Louisiana Tech, he supported me."

"What happened?"

"The head of the department and I had artistic differences. Your father told me not to compromise my viewpoint. He offered me this job until things get settled at the university."

"That explains a lot of things," Cindi said. "I've often had disagreements with my students over the interpretation of a particular piece of music. Are you going back when the thing is resolved?"

"Maybe, maybe not."

"What did 'our' father suggest?"

"He thinks I should go back."

"What do your own parents say?"

"They're too busy saving the heathen in Mexico to even know what's going on with me."

"Your parents are missionaries?"

"Yeah. When I was a kid, Dad had a church there and served as a missionary pastor. Then when I got older, my mother thought I needed to be here to get my schooling so they came back to Ida to live. But they couldn't get their love for those people out of their blood and went back to Mexico every chance they got."

"Did you enjoy living in Mexico when you were little?"

Dell shrugged. "It was all right. The kids there are like those anywhere else. Playing with them got me to speaking Spanish like a native. Miss Flowers likes that. We talk together in her native tongue often."

They both lapsed into silence then; Cindi sensed sincere regard for her father's opinion in Dell's words. She wondered again at her father's paradoxical nature. When she was young and needy, he'd left her to the care of her spoiled, childish mother. Now years later, he'd taken on an unrelated, needy, young person to nurture. But she couldn't feel slighted or jealous of Dell. She was glad her father had helped him.

CHAPTER 4

"La cucaracha, la cucaracha."

Rita's loud, tuneless voice penetrated Cindi's dream-filled sleep. She groaned at the harsh foreign words and pulled her pillow over her head to muffle the overly enthusiastic racket.

Who wants to hear a song about cockroaches so early in the morning?

The accompaniment to the unmelodic singing, a cacophony of banging and clattering pots and pans, intruded through the feather pillow. Cindi gave up on getting back to sleep, sitting up in bed to stretch.

"I thought this would be a peaceful, quiet getaway," she muttered to herself. "Only Cliff could find someone like Rita to 'help' me."

Cindi hated to wake up. Waking would mean letting go of her dream. A satisfying dream in which Dell held her as he had in the little country church. Lingering drowsiness left her, and Dell's muscled physique faded from her mind. She sighed. Already she could hardly remember what she'd dreamed. It was surely a reflection of what really happened yesterday only with added caresses and kisses. The tingle she'd felt in her dream from Dell's touch faded from her mind against her will.

In her relaxed state, Cindi was unafraid to face her growing attraction to Dell. After all, she'd only been dreaming. So what if he was younger than she? Who could be held accountable for subconscious thoughts?

She dragged herself from her comfortable bed, and found her way to the large, lavish bathroom. There, she opted for the whirlpool tub, though the completely furnished room boasted a Jacuzzi shower as well. Plunging into the warm, soothing water she hoped to pump vigor into her weary, still jet-lagged body. She pushed knobs until all the jets were at optimum operation. She luxuriated in the water's agitated movement around her sore body. The rushing sound muted the kitchen's sounds as well.

Cindi purred with pleasure.

She was sure Dell was busy performing that spectacular routine she'd surprised him at yesterday. The one he'd claimed as his regular, every-morning-without-fail exercise. Whatever, Cindi thought. It probably is. His body is supple and slim as a spring sapling while mine is untrained and overgrown like an unpruned camellia bush. I've always spent much more time training my vocal muscles.

She stepped from the tub, and the mirrored walls reflected her ample curves. She pummeled her hips and thighs, wishing the pounding would shake away some of the fat.

She shrugged. "No way that's going to happen," she said aloud to her reflection. A trip to the walk-in closet left her perplexed. The shorts and blouse she'd planned to wear weren't hanging where she thought they should be. She chose others, pale yellow shorts and a midriff top. Next, her hairbrush showed up in a different spot than she expected.

"I can't even remember where I've put things," she scolded inwardly. "The stress of Mother's death and Father's disappearance is affecting me more than I thought."

Hastily, she pulled her long, pale tresses back into a ponytail, and fastened that on the side of her head, making an offside topknot. Splashing water over her face, and adding light coral lipstick, she called her toilette done.

She'd hurried to the kitchen, meaning to spend quality time with Rita today. Today she wouldn't allow the woman to ramble on with tales about her homeland and its treasures. Today she meant to learn any and all facts about her father Rita might have.

The chat shouldn't cause her throat much pain because she already knew Rita was a woman of many words, albeit quite a few of them Spanish. *My guess is, we'll have a mind-boggling conversation because Spanish has never been my language of choice.*

As Cindi entered the kitchen, she trotted out one of the few Spanish phrases she knew. "*Buenas dias,* Rita. Your singing and the clatter of pots and pans woke me. I decided breakfast might be quite a production. What are we having?"

"Nothing much," Rita answered carelessly. "It is just my way in the kitchen to sing and bang around. I hope I did not disturb your rest too soon." Her tone suggested it really didn't matter much if she had.

"The food smells too heavenly not to be special," Cindi said.

"Well, I fix your father's favorites, eggs scrambled with hot peppers and onions. I have also cooked *tostados de maiz*—I think you would call them corn pancakes. And the coffee I make came with me straight from Colombia. I smuggle it through customs."

"That all sounds wonderful, uh, I mean the menu, not the smuggling," Cindi clarified. "The illegal coffee no doubt was hand picked by Juan Valdez. Don't I smell hot chocolate as well?"

"Oh, that is *chocolate santafereno*, very good and good for you," Rita claimed. "I make it especially for Dell. He looks as if he needs rich food. Eet is made with cream instead of milk. Who is thez Juan Valdez, Miss Cindi? I don't believe I know him."

"Oh never mind. I was trying for a little humor. This rich food can't hurt Dell, but with both of you cooking so many wonderful things to eat, I'm sure to gain ten pounds in no time flat."

At that moment, Dell came up behind her. Moving silently as usual on bare feet, he encircled Cindi's bare waist with his long slender hands. She gasped and jumped as goose bumps pebbled her arms even though warmth flushed her body at the same time.

"Ten pounds would only add to your charm, ma'am," he gallantly stated as he pulled her against his taut body.

"Hah, you shouldn't try to make me laugh. That's not good for my throat," Cindi fussed as she struggled to free herself and move away, despite the electric tingle she felt at every point of contact.

After she succeeded in getting away, she found a seat at the kitchen table. "Come on, Rita. Sit with us and have a cup of coffee. Tell us all about my father."

"*Si, senorita*, I will be glad to do that. I like your father. *Senor* Jim make me a good boss," Rita began as she took a seat.

Her glossy, dark brown hair, once more confined in its workaday coronet, shone in the sunlight streaming in from above. But the overhead lighting gave her dark eyes a malevolent gleam as she continued to speak.

"*Senor* Jim, he like to play tricks on us, the ones who work for him. He hide his clothes so we couldn't find them to wash. He claim it is because he always leave stuff in his pockets that we forget to remove.

"Sometimes when I straighten his room, I would find little pictures he draw for us. Sometimes he write on them. They are things he want us to do. I bring some with me. Would you like to see them?"

"Of course I would," Cindi answered. "Sounds like you enjoyed working for my father."

"I truly did, *Senorita*. As I already say, he is good boss. Many in my country would kill to have such a one."

As Rita left the room, Dell scooted his chair nearer Cindi. Cindi's nerves began to tingle again. Already his unexpected caress on her waist had reawakened the emotions of her early morning dream. Now he was acting as if he were attracted to her as well.

Jumping up from the table to escape the close quarters he'd maneuvered her into, she opened the door to the atrium. She stepped into the fragrant, enclosed space and glanced back over her shoulder. "I've never actually been into this garden yet."

Dell rose and followed her. Walking close together, they followed the narrow paths within the indoor garden.

So much for escaping temptation. He took my backwards glance as a "come hither."

"Who cares for the plants?" she asked, trying for a friendly, yet reserved, attitude.

"Me. That's part of my job description," Dell said. "Miss Flowers left me full instructions. You should be glad she didn't ask you to do it."

"Why?"

"Because most are native to her country. Imported with special permission from customs, some had to stay quarantined for months before she could have them. Most of them are rain forest plants. They need water at their roots and misting of their leaves every day. There'd surely be nothing but dry, brown stalks left if you were the gardener."

"I hate to admit that's true," Cindi answered his criticism. "I've thought I saw someone—or something—in here several times. It must have been you."

"Probably. Though it could have been Cordelia. Or even Delia, the Loggy Branch monster."

Dell's last offhand remark caught her unawares. "Cordelia? Who's she?" she asked. "And what is the Loggy Branch monster? A monster called Delia?"

"Cordelia is one of our resident ghosts. And the Loggy Branch monster is just an amusing legend the locals dreamed up. So they gave it an amusing name."

"You mean like a tale to encourage tourists to come or something?"

"Yeah, I guess. There's a festival and everything. A celebration for the monster. The kids enjoy it."

"And this Cordelia—is she the woman whose tombstone you stood staring at such a long time yesterday? I guess you're saying it's her ghost that haunts the place." Cindi let her voice deepen into a creepy note. If Dell meant to try to scare her at every turn, she'd give back as good as she got. "What does Cordelia mean to you anyway?"

Dell shot her a dangerous look. "I'd rather not talk about her."

Cindi stared back, wondering at his secretive manner. "Why not? You mentioned her first."

Dell looked uncomfortable. "Not now, okay?"

"Sorry, I didn't mean to trespass. Tell me instead how long it's taken you to learn all about the plants. How long have you been working here?"

"Apology accepted. I've been working here about a year. My parents have a house in town but they're gone on a missionary trip. I've always felt as if Mr. Jim and Miss Flowers were my foster parents anyway, so it just made sense to come here after I was put on academic suspension."

Just then Rita stepped into the atrium. "So that's how you get this job. But I never hear *Senor* Jim speak of you. Were you here when he left?"

"Sure I was. Mr. Jim is my hero," Dell answered simply.

Cindi wondered why Rita's nosy questions didn't cause the same offense hers had, but held her peace.

"Come see what I bring," Rita invited. "The pictures are on the kitchen table."

They all stepped back into the kitchen. Cindi examined the pictures, hoping for some insight into her father's mind. She felt certain her father had drawn them, so they gave credence to Rita's claim of working for him, knowing him.

"These are very amusing, but they don't help me any," Cindi said with a sigh. "He used to draw pictures like this for me when I was little. The letters he sent later often had some in their margins. I recognize them as his work, and his handwriting."

Many of the sketches were of a woman with Rita's distinctive hairdo. Doggerel verse on many exhorted the performance of some household task, but many were written in Spanish and Cindi didn't know exactly what they meant. One sketch pictured the woman differently. This figure was more richly dressed, wore earrings and bangle bracelets. Instead of a broom or duster, she carried a handbag. Under this figure was a single word, prim.

"May I borrow one or two of these to keep while I'm here?" Cindi asked Rita. "I'd like to have them in my room so I can look at them often. They'd make me feel closer to Father."

"But of course, *Senorita*. Take all if you wish," the maid agreed, a little too quickly and obsequiously. Her grudging tone belied her gracious words.

"Thanks, but I think these two are all I want," Cindi said, as she chose the one labeled "prim" and another one which showed the woman cooking.

As Cindi made her choices, Rita asked in a more spiteful voice, "Was last night's rest peaceful for you? I hear nothing, but sometimes I sleep like the dead."

"Yeah," Dell chimed in. "I keep forgetting to ask if you're getting any rest at nights. Have you seen or heard anything spooky yet?"

At Dell's words, the loose tendrils on Cindi's nape prickled and rose. She realized she'd never told him about the midnight concert. "Since that second night, things have been quiet," she said. "But then, I never told you what happened that night, did I?"

"You sure didn't. Tell me now."

"It was spooky enough. I was so scared, I screamed. It all started when I thought I heard someone in my room. Then just a little latter, about midnight, I heard the piano. Someone was playing Debussy's *Claire de Lune*. We had bright moonlight that night and it seemed such an appropriate choice. At first I wasn't scared, just curious about the identity of the player."

"You should have told me this before," Dell scolded. "Not that it makes much sense. You're sure it was *Claire de Lune?* That's one of Miss Flowers' favorite pieces. I recognize the name. I've heard her play it lots of times. What happened next?"

"From my room, I could see someone sitting at the piano, but not clearly. When I started to get up, the music stopped and the figure sitting there disappeared," Cindi continued obligingly.

"That was spooky! No wonder you were scared. Is that the only odd thing you've heard or seen?"

"I've already asked you about anyone who might have been in the atrium," Cindi said. "That's because several times I've thought I saw someone there."

"Cordelia!" Dell interjected.

"Whoever," said Cindi dismissively. "But there is something else. When I turned the lights on and went to the piano, I found one of the miniature pianos from Consuelo's collection had been placed on top of the real Steinway. When I picked it up, I looked down and saw a gleaming crimson spot on the Steinway's keys. I touched it and raised my hand to examine it. By the scent, I could tell it was blood. That's when I screamed and Rita came downstairs."

She looked at Rita, seeking confirmation of her story. The South American woman had been uncharacteristically quiet. So quiet, Cindi had almost forgotten her presence. As she glanced at her, the worried expression on the maid's face struck her as odd and out of place. Before she could even wonder about it, Dell spoke.

"I don't know anyone else who's had a midnight concert. Especially with a vanishing pianist. Sounds like you had one weird experience."

"That's the way it seemed to me," Cindi agreed as she continued to wonder why Rita still hadn't added her two cents worth.

"Most times the disturbances in the night are just a woman crying out the name, Delia. Miss Flowers swears she's seen her in the atrium as well."

"I didn't hear anything else," Cindi reiterated and shook her head for emphasis. "There weren't any other sounds and the only person I saw was the one at the keyboard. Other than the glimpses of some slim form in the atrium, that is. So that must be what Miss Flowers saw."

"The drop of blood and the piano tells me you didn't imagine the concert," Dell said. "And I keep telling you, Cordelia still walks in Magnolia House. Looks like you and Miss Flowers have both seen her."

As Dell spoke these words, Rita finally came to life. "Cordelia? Who is this Cordelia, you claim is here? If she is a spirit, say this is not true." Her face looked agitated and her voice sounded worried.

"All he's saying is just his opinion," Cindi said in an attempt to soothe the woman. "It's all just Dell's opinion. There's bound to be some much more logical explanation for all this."

Rita's face relaxed into a less troubled look. "*Madre Dios,* let it be so. Let it be as you say, Miss Cindi," she breathed with fervor.

"I'm sure I'm right," Cindi said. "Let's hear about the spooky things you've seen around here Dell. I'll bet you can't think of a single one, can you? And if you haven't seen anything, how can you claim this ghost really exists or appears or whatever? And how can you claim to know who it is?" Cindi continued in an incredulous tone. Even to herself, she sounded a little disappointed. She also realized she'd resorted to one of her favorite tactics, non-stop, incessant questions.

Dell looked taken aback by her aggressive behavior. "I really have never seen anything," he admitted. "I claimed I had because I wanted you to take me seriously. I have heard a coarse voice cursing and hollering about 'the black cat.' And I have heard a woman crying, crying and calling the nickname Delia."

At this, both Cindi and Rita began to pay rapt attention. Both waited anxiously to hear what Dell might say next.

"*Madre Dios,* why didn't anyone tell me this place is haunted? I would have stayed far away from it. And you say you hear these voices, Dell?" Rita asked, as her expression grew worried once more.

"Well, Cordelia was my girl friend's name. She was killed in a wreck near here about three years ago," Dell began to explain. His voice was even huskier than usual, his face contorted as if he might cry. "We were driving near here. All at once a big cat like the locals call a 'painter' showed up right in the middle of the road and I swerved to miss it. I didn't know how to drive well enough to regain control of my car and we hit a tree. I always figured the cat was the panther folks call the 'monster of Loggy Branch.' The really strange thing is that they also claim the panther is female and sometimes they call her Delia."

As Cindi tried to console Dell, she heard Rita moaning something about "el tigre."

"I'm so sorry that happened to you," she said looking at Dell. Until he'd added the last about his girl friend's death, she'd been nearly convinced he was making up all this ghostly stuff just to scare her and Rita. His sad story gained her sympathy and convinced her of his sincerity.

She suffered a perverse pang of jealousy over the dead girl as she remembered that grave marked with Cordelia's name. Dell had spent a long time in silence before that grave.

"Yeah, thanks," Dell said. "But let's not dwell on sadness that's past and gone. Let's find something else to talk about or something fun to do. How about a swim in the pool? I just cleaned it. The water should be nice."

Cindi was sure she would enjoy the cool water. She wasn't sure she could bear Dell's scrutiny of her plump body in a revealing swimsuit.

She knew that would make her very self-conscious. In fact, just the quizzical expression on his face as she tried to decide how to answer him, made her nerves jumpy.

"Oh well, what the hey, it'll be a good thing to do on a hot summer day," she finally burst out in unconscious rhyme. "Rita, why don't you join us?"

Her last plea came in the hope that Rita's voluptuous body would divert Dell's attention from her own. Besides Rita's expression was oddly forlorn as if she needed cheering as well. But the South American's breezy way with words doomed Cindi's hopes.

"I have too many things to do this morning," Rita said. "But if I get through, I'll come jump in and join you. Thank you for asking me, *Senorita.*"

CHAPTER 5

"Ooh, why did I ever agree to a swim in the pool? I wonder which swimsuit I can wear. I need one that covers up as much of me as possible, so it certainly won't be this pink bikini or this blue one either," Cindi muttered as she tossed skimpy bits of fabric over her shoulder onto the floor. All the while she wondered why none of her belongings were exactly where she expected them to be.

"Ah," she breathed as she dug out a black one-piece suit with a high halter-top. Quickly she eased into the suit and approved her mirrored reflection.

This one makes me look ten pounds lighter and is about as covered up as a swimsuit can be.

She pulled out the suit's matching sheer, polka dot cover-up to wear while out of the water. Then she pulled her long hair into a ponytail, loosely piled it on top of her head and fastened it there securely with special long hairpins that had belonged to her Grandmother St. Germaine. She draped the black and white cover-up over her shoulders and ventured out to the pool.

When she arrived at poolside, Dell was already sporting around in the water. With his long hair slicked back and glistening, his head looked sleek as a seal's. When he saw Cindi, he shook the water from his face and hair, climbed out and mounted the diving board. The water formed glistening drops on his tan, muscled torso. Cindi eyed his form, as perfect as a Michelangelo statue come to life, then dropped her head in confusion.

As she searched for something—anything else—to focus on, Tai caught her attention. There he was, lying on the grass under a lantana bush. Cindi smiled at the sight. Dell's lion dog had apparently scoped out an out-of-the-way spot where he would be free from random splashes.

His tail and hindquarters waggled furiously in welcome as Cindi went over to give him the petting he expected. As she brushed against the lantana's cheerful yellow and orange flowers, the bush's pungent scent filled the air. She could hear Dell's urging from the pool.

"Come on in, the water's fine. It will make you feel divine. You will soon feel so good, you'll treat me exactly as you should." Pause, then a further gibe. "Ma'am."

Cindi looked back at Dell from the shelter of the lantana bush. Dell's words gave her a funny feeling. A premonition that he was going to be hard to handle this afternoon.

"So now you've become a poet—and a nonsense poet at that. I'd like to know just what kind of nonsense you're spouting anyway. Sir." Cindi issued her demand with the false courage that she had been using quite often lately.

Dell now floated on his back, a stream of water worthy of a mighty whale spurting from his mouth. He didn't answer.

"I've always treated you exactly as I should—with complete respect and friendliness," Cindi continued, approaching the pool with caution, expecting him to splash her at any moment. "What do you expect other than that?"

Dell flipped over and swam to the side of the pool. "You'd better not call my words of wisdom nonsense. Besides, no one ever said I wanted respect from you. Actually, what I want is more—uh, I guess you could call it friendliness." He gave her an intense look as she paused on the edge.

"Yeah, more friendliness," he added. "From you, you great looking babe, uh, lady."

She fended off his hands as he attempted to drag her in the water by her ankles. "So that's what you want. I might be able to oblige. But only if you'd treat me like the lady you say I am, because what I want is respect."

She felt sparks ignite from his playful touches and sensed the hidden meanings flowing beneath their bantering words. She eased out of her sheer jacket, and as quickly as possible slid into the pool and into the concealing water.

At first she carefully steered clear of Dell. He seemed anxious to stay clear of her as well. Perhaps he remembered as she did the fusion of their hands when he'd helped her cross Loggy Branch. Perhaps they both remembered the comforting way he'd held her in the church.

"That's the most sensational covered-up bathing suit I've ever seen," Dell said, swimming closer at last.

"Why thank you, kind sir," Cindi answered. "I always try to please."

"There you go, giving me some more of that respect. I thought I told you I want none of that stuff," Dell said as he reached out and circled her wrists with his hands, drawing her inexorably closer.

"Wait a minute, now."

"Oh, shut up and come here," Dell said.

Cindi realized he was going to kiss her. As he placed his lips on hers, they were cool and wet. But his kiss soon turned sizzling hot as the tremors it evoked sped along Cindi's nerves and set her face aglow. She pulled away and began to swim to the side of the pool.

She felt sure he would only let her get so far before he'd catch her again. She was right, and the ducking, splashing and general rough housing began in earnest then. She tried to quell her ambivalent feelings for him, but each chance touch built the seething emotion Cindi tried to control. Each word Dell spoke seemed to carry some extra meaning she searched for ardently.

"Beat you to the other end of the pool," Dell finally challenged.

The race was on. After a grueling impromptu sprint the length of the pool and back several times, Cindi had to drag herself out to rest. She grabbed her robe as soon as she got out and flung it on.

"I give," she said. "This lady is beat." She winced as Dell jumped out as well and sat down on a large beach towel beside her lounge chair. Now he was closer than ever. He captured her right hand and began to massage and caress her supple, sensitive fingers. Shivers of feeling flowed over her as Dell rubbed them. The response passed to her face and set it aflame.

Tai's full-fledged barks drew their attention from each other. Dell rose to quiet the dog as Cliff strode out of the house and down to the pool.

"Rita told me I'd find you here, Cindi," he said in a false, hearty voice. "I hope I'm not pushing my way in where I'm not wanted."

"Of course you aren't," Cindi denied, pulling her body and chair up to a more erect position. She also adjusted her cover-up, which had fallen open. "I'd like you to meet Dell Comeaux, Consuelo's caretaker," she added as Dell returned from the pool house where he had taken Tai.

Cliff completely ignored her introduction of Dell. "You should be wearing a hat. Your face looks as if you may have gotten a little too much sun," he said, drawling out his words while studying her still-burning face.

"This Louisiana sun could never burn a California girl like me," she retorted, seething at the man's deliberate lack of response to her introduction of Dell.

"You have turned into a tanned beach babe since you left this state," Cliff affirmed. "California seems to have been good for you." His husky voice made the words into a sensuous purring compliment.

Cindi, at a loss for the right way to answer Cliff's continued impertinence, could see Dell's face turning a dark, purplish color. She could see his fists clenching and unclenching as he struggled to keep from doing damage to the other man. She got up from her chair and moved away to pace the edge of the pool. Cliff merely sat back and showed complacent amusement at their mutual discomfort.

"What do you want?" Cindi finally croaked.

"Yes, answer the lady's question," Dell added. "What do you want and what are you doing here?"

Cliff never took his gaze from Cindi, but he did respond to Dell's question. "I've come to discuss private business with the lady."

"Go ahead with what you've got to say. Don't mind me. I'm just one of the hired hands," Dell interjected in a voice that came out harsh and tight.

"Now you're being silly, Dell," Cindi appeased. "I've already told Cliff you're too independent to be considered hired help. I never think of you that way. Certainly Cliff and I can talk right here."

But Cliff objected by saying in a warning tone, "This concerns your father's release and the conditions that must be met before we can secure it. But if you're sure about Dell, there's no reason to go anywhere else to talk about it."

Dell drew himself up from the seat he'd resumed on return from the pool house. In a single sinuous move, he was up and marching back toward his house before she could say a word.

Cindi didn't know what to do. She was afraid of hurting Dell's sensitive feelings even more by rushing after him. She was also reluctant to be alone with Cliff. Drat the man. He made her feel like the untried teenager she'd been when they became engaged.

"Dell, don't go," she cried, but it was too late. He had already reached the pool house without a backward glance and only the slightest wave of his hand for goodbye.

"You have quite a lot of feelings for a young good-for-nothing like that," Cliff commented smoothly.

"You shouldn't pronounce judgment on people you don't even know. Dell is a young artist my father has been helping," Cindi began hotly. She stopped herself as she realized she was playing right into Cliff's hands by defending Dell. She also saw the lust-filled look in Cliff's eyes signifying her display of temper interested him.

"Okay, okay, I apologize. I had forgotten that passionate loyalty you give wholeheartedly to your friends," Cliff said with uplifted hands and a deprecating laugh as he continued to study her.

Cindi stonily returned his stare. He was still one of the most drop-dead-handsome men she'd ever seen. No wonder she had fallen so hard at age seventeen when he first flattered her with his attention.

His sulky mouth, half-hidden by his luxuriant beard and mustache, invited bold kisses. Cindi felt shame rise because in her younger days, she had done that. Before she found out he was using her infatuation as an ego booster. Cindi had believed herself in love with the man. Only his eventual rejection of her had shown her that imagined love was false.

Her cheeks warmed and she imagined them burning even more brightly at her recollections. She tightly folded her arms over her chest and lifted her chin haughtily as she faced him. Now her only feeling for him was dislike.

"Please go on with what you came here to tell me," she insisted.

"All right. I'll give it to you straight. The people who have your father want a ransom of $200,000 for his release. That's American money. The deadline for delivery of the cash is two days from now."

"I don't have access to that kind of money. I thought Consuelo was to handle the money part. I thought she was there in the country to deal with the people who have my father—the government or whoever. What is she doing? Where is she?" Cindi's voice grew weaker and weaker as she turned away from Cliff in despair.

How could she help her father? She thought she might actually die from the crushing blow Cliff had handed her hopes for her father's safety.

"Consuelo has disappeared herself. She hasn't been seen since she got on the plane for South America."

Cindi turned back to stare at Cliff in stunned disbelief. If this were so, there was no way to secure her father's release. Her own inheritance from her mother was hopelessly bound up in legalities and conditions. It would be months before the will even cleared probate. In the meantime, her own income would have to stretch to take care of her day-to-day expenses.

"We'll find a way around the terms of your mother's will," Cliff said in a silken tone as if he could read her mind. He approached closer and held out his arms.

With hands raised to ward him off, Cindi hissed in her small remnant of a voice, "Don't touch me. Don't even come near me. If I didn't need you to negotiate my father's release, I'd tell you to leave and never ever come back. Do you understand me?"

"I understand. You are the one who doesn't seem to understand. I'm only trying to help you."

"The only way you can help is by getting my father out of that country and back here. Let me get my lawyer's phone number. You can talk to him the next time you have anything to report. I want nothing else to do with you."

Cindi shook with anger and fear as she dashed away from the man and into her room to get her lawyer's number. When she returned, she flung a small piece of paper at him saying, "Here. Here's the number. Call my lawyer next time. Stall the people in Colombia. Tell them we need more time to get the money. And until you've done that, stay away from me and Magnolia House. Now you'd better leave."

As she uttered those last words, Cindi turned toward the pool. Ripping off her cover-up, she dove in with a mighty splash. She swam away to the other side of the water, ignoring his loud protests.

* * *

Inside the atrium, Dell heard voices in the hall. As he knelt behind a large, blooming pyracantha bush, transplanting seedlings, he was completely hidden from view. Through the branches and blossoms of the showy, thorny bush, he saw Rita and Cliff in the foyer with their arms around each other. He stilled his movements and hunkered closer to the dirt of the flowerbed. His view was excellent, but he could only hear an occasional tantalizing word.

"You... Mr. Jim?...think Cindi...money?"

These words were uttered in Rita's grating tones.

"...good...she can...use it." Cliff's oily cadence sounded next.

"Dell…too nosy." This came from Rita.

Dell crawled unobtrusively closer, taking care to keep cover between himself and the couple. Their words irritated him. He wanted to hear what Rita said about him, but by the time he got close enough to hear, she was talking about Cindi again.

"…keep on trying to scare Cindi away?"

"Sure, we need to use this place. It's a shame she had to turn up here. And you keep looking for Consuelo's treasure stash. We need all the money we can get our hands on to handle my campaign for governor."

"Yes, I help you, Cliff. When you are governor, I will be First Lady of Louisiana. At last I will have my rightful place. No more serving in the kitchen. I will be the lady I was born to be."

Dell watched as Rita wound her arms more tightly around Cliff, and the couple began to kiss. There were no more words then, only rustlings and sighs. Dell lowered his head in disgust, unable to watch.

His mind raced. Had Cliff and Rita expected Magnolia House to be empty? What treasure was Rita looking for? Did Rita really imagine herself a lady?

As he pondered these things, he let his gaze wander absently over the garden. He sought spots that needed weeding or pruning and found them. Good, he would have plenty of work as soon as Cliff left. His hands busy, his mind would be free to puzzle over Cliff and Rita's words.

CHAPTER 6

"I'm going to town," Dell said while they ate lunch. He spied Cindi's red eyes and the puffiness around them. He was sure Cliff's news had caused her grief, and thought she needed a diversion. "Why don't you come, too?"

"Is Tai going?" Cindi asked as Rita cleared the table. "If Tai goes, I'll go."

"Sure, Tai's going. Makes me happy you think so much of him. Remember the old saying, if you love my dog, you gotta love me."

With a small chuckle, Cindi refuted that. "I think you've got that old saying a little mixed up. It's love me, love my dog. And besides, just because your dog is an easy-to-love sweetheart doesn't mean a thing when it comes to his master."

As she finished, Cindi looked up teasingly at Dell. "Just the same, I'll tag along with you and your dog," she agreed.

Thoughts of Dell distracted Cindi as she left the kitchen to get her purse. She wished she read him as easily as she did his dog. If so, she might trust him more. Could he be exactly what he claimed to be? A young man her father and Consuelo had helped over a difficult time? Or, did they even know of his presence at Magnolia House?

After all, Cliff had seemed surprised to find Dell here. Plus, Consuelo had never mentioned him to her. Cindi's own bad judgment in men, especially her terrible mistake in Cliff, caused her to stop short of complete trust in Dell.

As the truck pulled out of the garage and headed down the mile-long driveway, Cindi's spirits lifted. Magnolia House was a luxurious, lovely, light-filled place, but leaving it removed an oppressive cloud from her mind. The atmosphere of the place held hidden secrets, strange shadows hovering just out of sight.

The bizarre midnight concert, the uneasy feeling someone had been rifling through her things, Cliff's repeated and continued, unexpected appearances—all these added together left her glad for a change of scene. She drew a breath of freedom as the truck moved through the gate to the property and headed south to town.

Every mile they traveled helped her grow move optimistic about her father's release. Soon she started to hum a tune. She opened her mouth to sing its words, then remembered her doctor's warning and shut it again without warbling a note.

"I'm having such a hard time not singing. Not talking much is no picnic either," she sighed. "Those two things are as natural as breathing to me."

"I'm sure I would feel about the same if I'd been told not to paint or play my guitar," Dell said.

Tai offered comfort in his own way. The dog moved his huge head over to Cindi's knee. Curled on the seat between them, he seemed to sense Cindi's need for sympathy.

"My father won't be released until we come up with a ransom of $200,000," she burst out as she scratched behind the dog's ears.

"Holy cow," Dell exploded. "That's a lot of money, but surely Miss Flowers will be able to put up the money with no problem. She's got plenty of cash."

"Whether she can or can't is a moot question. She's disappeared. Cliff told me this morning that no one has seen her since he took her to board the plane."

"So that's what he said that made you cry. I've never seen that guy until that day he came to see you. I don't believe him."

"Are you sure? Could you have missed him when he came? He seems perfectly at home around Magnolia House."

"What do you mean, am I sure? Believe me, I'm sure, trust me."

Trust. That's exactly what Cindi had been struggling with, so she answered, "I'm not sure what to believe myself. Or whom to trust."

A strained silence settled over the cab of the truck. Tai whined uneasily. Cindi pouted. Dell drove with every sense trained on the road.

"I heard Cliff and Rita talking, saw them in a clench, kissing," he finally offered.

"Cliff and Rita?" Cindi's voice was questioning.

"Yeah. I went over to the atrium to work on the plants after I left you and Cliff at the poolside. I had to do something physical or explode. After a while I heard voices. I'm ashamed to say I stayed behind the bushes and scooted close enough to make out words. They didn't see me behind all the foliage."

"Okay," Cindi encouraged.

"They were talking about money and about the house," Dell began. Then he went on to tell Cindi the bits and pieces he'd heard.

Cindi shook her head over the part of Cliff running for governor. She decided to put her trust in Dell. She was sure he'd never make up anything so absurd. "So you're telling me, Rita's been the one going through my stuff and maybe staging the scary things I've seen and heard. I've been thinking it might be you."

Dell gave a snort of laughter and shook his head. "I would really feel ashamed if I sunk that low. Besides, I keep telling you, I wouldn't care if you stayed at Magnolia House forever, babe. So I'm not about to try to scare you off."

Cindi disregarded his protest. But she nodded her head thoughtfully, as a look of acceptance grew stronger on her face. "I think I believe you," she said slowly as if thinking aloud. "After all, Cliff was surprised when I told him about you. And Rita's had every chance to go through the master suite and meddle with things. I still don't understand how she set up the piano playing, though. And what they wanted to use Magnolia House for in the first place."

"Those are all good questions. This treasure they're looking for must be something pretty valuable. And Magnolia House's location would be good for smuggling dope or whatever."

"Yes, it's secluded enough," Cindi said. "So you think those two are behind everything? I wish I could believe that."

"I guess we're back to the trust thing. You're still not sure who to believe. Trust me, babe. Rely on me, just let yourself go, and believe me. You can, you know, but I'm not sure anyone—even Rita—can believe anything Cliff says."

Cindi knew from past experience that was true. "You mean he could have been lying to me about my father. And Consuelo? And even lying to Rita. Yes, that's the Cliff I know and once thought I loved."

The moment she finished speaking, she regretted her tongue's slip.

"I thought that old guy had a thing for you," Dell said as a satisfied smile lit his face.

"I'm not sure how he felt, but I thought he was the man for me once. Even planned to marry him, until I found out he really didn't mean to go that far."

"Were you two engaged to be married?"

"Yes," Cindi admitted. "But I think I really pressured him into the whole thing. All that was over long ago. Now he's just my father's partner."

"Isn't he a little old for you?"

"That was a lot of his attraction for me. I thought it was wonderful when he began to pay attention to me. In fact, that blinded me to his true nature, the snake."

"He still thinks you're attracted to him, even while he's stringing Rita along."

"Cliff thinks he's God's gift to women and that every woman is instantly attracted to him. Let's get back to Father and Consuelo. How do we know she's really disappeared? The only indication of it, other than the fact that I haven't heard a word from her since I got here, comes from Cliff."

"She could have just gone under cover. Maybe she doesn't trust Cliff either," Dell said. "I'm sure no one in Colombia would mess with the Delgado family."

"She's connected to the Delgado's? I thought her father had made his fortune in coffee," Cindi asked, suitably impressed. Even she had heard of that legendary, Colombian family of wealth and political power, reputed as well to have ties to the Emerald Mafia who controlled the emerald mining.

"The Delgado's are her mother's people. Miss Flowers' parents divorced while she was here in the state going to college. After she graduated from LSU, she went back to Colombia and lived with her mother. She finally came back to Louisiana when her father died and she inherited this property."

"And that's when she and Father got together again. I'm getting depressed all over. Let's forget all this for now."

"Suits me. I'll distract you by being your tour guide and tell you about all the sights."

At Cindi's nod, Dell began his spiel. "Now coming up on your left is historic St. Elisabeth Church which you've already visited. I hope you remember that visit," he said with a meaningful look at her. "And now coming up to your right is the one-time scandal of the northern part of Caddo Parish, Spoonful Bar. 'Come to Spoonful and get a snoot full' was its motto. In its day, this was a place of ill-repute where a man could get dead drunk or even truly dead with equal odds."

"How did such a place come to be built so near the church?" Cindi asked, puzzled over the two diverse buildings situated catty-corner from each other and separated only by the gravel road. A high-banked curve obscured the view from one to the other, however. "The church members probably couldn't actually see the bar, but the noise coming from it would be hard to ignore."

"This used to be the biggest settlement in north Caddo Parish. You know every community needs places for sinners, at least one to practice in, plus at least one to repent in. I guess the old timers just built those places near each other."

"And the good Lord must have shared my opinion that they were too close," Cindi said. "St. Elisabeth Church stands four square and straight as ever and Spoonful's nothing but ruins now. I can imagine how it must have looked once, though."

As they passed, Cindi could almost see the parking lot full of battered pick up trucks, old jalopies and the overflow of drunken people from the bar. Loud music spilled out as well. Age-old raucous laughter and bawdy words seemed to quiver in the air. Passion, inflamed by liquor, would run high among the shadowy crowd she sensed there.

A premonitory chill ran down her back and raised the hair on her arms. She shivered involuntarily. The mournful cooing cry of a dove sounded through the open windows of the truck and became an echo of the imagined past. A hot fetid breeze blew through along with it. The odor of cheap perfume and alcohol fumes and the rich, salty smell of fresh-spilt blood rode in on it.

"I've got another tale about old Spoonful", Dell said.

"What's that?"

"How the roadhouse got its name. You see back in those boom days, whiskey was so expensive it sold by the spoonful is what I've been told."

Cindi suddenly found herself enjoying the trip again. Dell's words tickled her, rousing her sense of humor. "Must have been some pretty wealthy sinners around then."

"You got that, babe. Guys filthy with oil, and filthy rich to boot. Now you need to forget all that and get your eyes peeled and ready, 'cause here comes town. It will perk you right up, but you have to be ready or you might just miss it."

Cindi chuckled over Dell's last words. They drove through the neat little town that indeed was very small. Only a few people were to be seen. Dell drove down Main Street and through some of the residential part. Well-kept homes sat in carefully tended yards testifying to the solid, steady people living in them. They passed the small schoolhouse and no less than three churches, one Baptist, one Catholic and one called, The Church of God.

"I would hardly think there were enough people in this little burg to fill one church much less three," Cindi commented.

"There's two or three more on the outskirts of town toward Shreveport, and you already know about St. Elisabeth's out by us," Dell said. "Maybe folks just feel the need for the Lord around here."

Cindi remained silent, remembering the uncontrolled violence she sensed had once existed at Spoonful Bar. She nodded in agreement.

Dell pulled up and parked in front of a store on the main street and turned to Cindi. "How about this? It's a genuine old-fashioned general store. Are you coming in with me?"

The store looked quaint and out-of-date to her. The large building's plate glass windows each bore the single word, "Hathaway's" and were bare of any displays of merchandise. A long wooden bench that looked as if it had once been a church pew from St. Elisabeth's stood near the front door. The place, definitely not bustling with business, looked dark and quiet inside.

"It's not much like Bullock's or even the smallest shops in the mall back home. I don't believe there's anything I need in there. Maybe I'll just visit the library. I see it's right next door," Cindi said.

The small, new looking building several feet from the store had caught her attention. The sign on it read North Caddo Memorial Library, Ida Branch.

"Yeah," she continued, as Dell remained silent. "I'll visit the store another day. I'll head over to find something to read. Just let me know when you're ready to leave."

Though Cindi tried to encourage him to follow her, Tai seemed torn between her and Dell. Finally the dog settled down in a shady patch. It was halfway between the two buildings that were the destinations of his favorite humans. Cindi watched as his head moved back and forth between her and Dell. His face set in a perplexed frown, and a worried furrow made his brows droop even more than usual.

"That's right, Tai. From this spot, you can watch both buildings and the truck." She almost laughed at the canine's wrinkled, furrowed face which betrayed his uneasiness as he looked up at her before curling into a tight ball to wait.

Cindi turned and entered the library. She was impressed with her first good look at the pristine interior, which smelled of new lumber as if recently built. She studied a small plaque near the front desk, which stated that the library had been built with funds donated by the estate of Matthew Flowers. The library had been dedicated July 18, 1991. Matthew must have been Consuelo's father, Cindi decided.

She strolled farther into the pleasant building and found it like no library she had ever visited before. It boasted a southern exposure of expensive glass bricks, which ran around the corner and extended to the door she had entered through. The shelves of books were freestanding and the whole place was light and airy.

She felt a thrill of recognition. She knew this work. She was sure her father had designed this building.

"May I help you?" a pleasant voice asked.

"Yes," Cindi said as she turned to look at the owner of the voice. She saw before her a middle-aged woman with a faded pretty face. Her lips were curved in a smile that didn't quite reach her uneasy, brown eyes. Those eyes held a world of trouble and sorrow. Cindi longed to open her arms to the woman so they could comfort each other.

"I'm Cindi Lynn. I'm new around here. I'm house sitting at Magnolia House. What I want to know is, are there any books about the history of this area?"

"There's a special section with books about Louisiana in general. I think there's one with the history of Caddo Parish. And there's another about this corner of the state which was known as 'no-man's land' back before Texas came into the Union." The librarian pointed out the direction to the books to Cindi. "I'm sure we can fix you up with a temporary library card, so you can check out any books that interest you," the woman finished.

Cindi's mind reeled. Before Texas came into the Union was a little further back than she intended to go in her study of the region.

As the librarian found the necessary forms for Cindi to fill out for a library card, she told Cindi her name was Samantha Carver.

"You must have met Dell Comeaux," Mrs. Carver remarked as she studied the information Cindi had given her. "Perhaps you've heard him speak of my daughter Cordelia. They're good friends."

Cindi moved toward the section the woman had pointed out. She didn't know what to say. The hair on her arms rose as her skin started prickling again. Chills traversed the length of her spine. Dell had told her Cordelia was dead, but Mrs. Carver was speaking of her as if she were still alive.

Choosing her books, Cindi's thoughts were chaotic. *Talk about small town gothic. This place is filled with folks who won't stay dead, strangely haunted living folks, and buildings filled with light, yet possessed by shadows.*

She'd decided against research books and settled on some romance novels written by Louisiana authors. She took her selections back to the desk. Before Cindi could decide what to say next to the librarian, Dell called from the door.

"Hi, Mrs. Carver," he said. "Are you helping Cindi find the books she wants? I'm through at the store and ready to go anytime now."

Cindi thanked Samantha Carver for her help. She hurriedly left the library, which now looked less open and pleasant than it had when she entered.

"Tell me about your girlfriend's mother," were her first words to Dell when they got into the truck. "Is she…all right?"

"Since you're asking, she must have talked about Cordelia," Dell said. "Everyone around here overlooks her when she starts that. We've decided it eases her pain to forget for a while that Cordelia is gone. Most of the time she doesn't talk that way."

"How does it make you feel when she does? I don't mean to pry or make you sad, but it must be especially hard for you when she refuses to face reality."

"Not really. Sometimes I'm not sure what reality is either."

Cindi could tell from Dell's expression that he wasn't going to add anything to his last statement. She mulled silently over it. She had to admit she wasn't sure of reality these days herself.

She'd learned today that some of the unearthly things she had witnessed had been staged to scare her, she was staying in a house where ghosts supposedly walked—and played piano. She had caught glimpses of a shadowy form at the piano and the atrium. All in all, the real world was becoming a little hard to define since she arrived at Magnolia House.

"When I left California, I had the strange idea I was coming here for a quiet, restful stay in the country. I thought this would be the perfect place to recover from my surgery—and my mother's death," she mused aloud, not caring what Dell thought. "After all, Consuelo made it sound that way. Somehow things aren't exactly the way I imagined they'd be."

"Is that good or bad?" Dell asked.

Cindi had to laugh. She decided to give Dell something of his own to puzzle over. "There are some very good things about my visit here, but there are a few very bad ones too. And that's all I'm going to say about that." The pleasant expression from her laughter remained on her face.

"Those good things must be very good, because you look as smug as the smuggest canary catcher I ever saw."

Cindi grinned. Neither Rita nor Dell had been part of her projected imaginings back in California, not to mention Cordelia's ghost. Now she couldn't imagine staying if Dell weren't around. He was the only one she knew had nothing to do with all the mysterious things she'd seen and heard.

With this in mind, she covertly studied Dell's aquiline profile as the miles passed. His long hair was drawn back in a neat ponytail today and tied with a leather thong. She supposed that was a concession to the trip to town. Without the tangle of hair close to his face, his strong features stood out even more. His appearance fascinated her. Longing to touch his face and trace each feature gently, she sighed.

As the truck passed St. Elisabeth Baptist Church and the little cemetery there, Cindi felt sorrow pierce her heart. Her mother's death settled there once more like a heavy burden only momentarily lifted. She sent up a swift prayer that she might be spared the loss of her father as well.

All too soon, they pulled into the garage at Magnolia House. Dell took Cindi's hand as he helped her down from the truck. He held her hand lightly afterward, then suddenly bent to kiss her with a passion that bordered on anger.

Cindi had dreamed of his kisses, but they'd been tender and yearning in her dream. Helplessly she opened her lips under the pressure of his. His tongue found the opening and she tasted it with her own as he ran it lightly over her lower lip. He tasted like the apple he had plucked from the grocery bag and eaten as he drove home. He tasted sweet and fresh and young.

She longed to melt into his body. She fit herself into the muscled hollows of his frame and drew closer as she pressed against him. Her heart racing, her breath short, she felt his parted lips leave her mouth and move down the column of her throat. Pausing at the soft, hollowed spot there at the base, he covered that spot with kisses turned gentle.

Her skin flamed. Her breasts felt turgid with desire. She arched her neck and closed her eyes at the delight she felt in his touch.

Dell had been gripping her upper arms and now encircled her body and drew her still closer. Her sensitive breasts were crushed against his chest. Sure there could be no more air in her lungs, she gasped and took in the scent of Dell's unique, fresh smell along with the air she needed. Like that air or the feel of sunshine on her skin, his scent was sweet and pure, necessary and perfect. But she knew this idea was madness so she pushed herself out of his arms and hurried into the house.

CHAPTER 7

Cindi stirred uneasily in the large bed, as some sound drew her out of the restless sleep she'd struggled to reach. The twisted sheets held her captive and thoughts of the trip she'd made to Ida with Dell filled her drowsy mind.

He seemed to enjoy being with me. I know I enjoyed being with him. Why did he leave so soon after we got back and unloaded the supplies? He didn't even show for supper either. That frosted Rita.

Disappointment colored Cindi's thoughts. Their last words had been spoken in the garage under the watchful eyes of Rita Gomez. Right after that kiss. That fateful kiss.

I guess he saw me on the deck moping around. I certainly could see him. He was working at the easel in the pool house. If he had wanted to come over, he would have. His precious art is more important than I am.

Good thing I had a book to read, Cindi thought as she slowly wakened fully. With sticky eyes and stuffy head, she wondered what she'd heard. She was sure it had been some unusual noise. She listened intently for it to come again.

There was plenty of noise. During the night, the wind had risen and blustered with an eerie sound against the skylights of Magnolia House. It tore through the leaves of the banana trees on the walled patio off the master suite and caused strange shadows on the bedroom wall.

As Cindi listened for the noise to repeat itself, rain started to pound down. It beat in sharp, staccato bursts on the large expanse of plexiglass over the atrium and the bath. Flashes of lightning lit the plants in the garden with a bluish, intermittent light. But she was sure neither the wind nor the first soft patters of rain had wakened her.

During a storm like this, Cindi usually snuggled deeper in her bed, content to be safe from the harsh elements outside. But this house let in so much of the outdoors that right now, she didn't feel safe or sheltered here in Magnolia House. Besides too many strange things had happened, especially the muted, ghostly voices and barely seen entities in the atrium.

"Delia… Delia," called a frightened, feminine voice.

So faint the sound, Cindi thought it the sigh of the wind at first. But this was the noise she had heard in her dreams. This was the sound that had wakened her.

The name was repeated over and over softly but insistently. Cindi thought what she heard could only come from a supernatural source. When the sound of uncontrolled, sorrowful weeping began, she trembled. Louder than the wind, louder than the volleys of rain, the cry of a soul in torment moved nearer.

Cindi huddled under her covers shaking and terrified. She pulled her pillow over her ears. Dell's taunting prediction that she would hear the ghost came to her.

Rita's upstairs. She's doing this to scare me. That's another thing Dell told me. This is just the kind of commotion she'd cause if she pretended to be the ghost. But it can't be her. No accent.

All this while, the frightened voice continued to sob and wail out the name Delia over and over. Now much nearer, a high-pitched shriek split the air. An unearthly shriek that couldn't have come from a human throat.

Cindi sat up in bed determined not to scar her throat by adding her own scream to the echoes of the one that had just sounded. She held her lips firmly closed refusing to let out the sound that grew there.

Instead, Rita screamed, "*El tigre! El tigre*!"

Then Cindi heard Rita's noisy sobs.

"I'm coming, Rita. Don't be afraid." Cindi whispered to herself as she rushed to Rita. In her haste to comfort the other woman, Cindi forgot her own fears. She scaled the stairs to the balcony to reach Rita's side. Before she could do more than put her arms around the woman, she heard another voice.

"Cindi, Rita, where are you? Are you all right?" Dell called from the foyer as he dropped his umbrella by the door. "I thought I heard a scream and I got over here as soon as I could."

Trembling and shaking, Cindi and Rita started down the stairs to meet Dell. He met them halfway.

"I'm so glad you're here," Cindi said to him. "Something weird is going on."

"From the way both of you are shaking, I'd say that was an understatement," Dell said. "What happened?"

Cindi and Rita began talking at the same time. Each tried to tell Dell of the woman's voice and the shriek that Rita insisted had come not from a woman but from "el tigre." They were both shaking from nerves and chilled, for the storm had lowered the warm outside temperatures so, the icy blasts from the air conditioning were suddenly too much.

Cindi couldn't help noticing that Rita's filmy sleepwear was attracting Dell's attention. Even frightened beyond words, the Colombian still looked sexy. "Rita, why don't you go back up and get your robe," she suggested.

"I borrow one of yours, Miss Cindi. I can't go back up there alone."

Dell waited outside Cindi's room as both women found warmer coverings. Then he led them into the den, the only room out of sight of the atrium. He went to the kitchen and returned shortly with cups of warm milk laced with brandy.

Rita spat hers out as soon as she tasted it. "Milk!" she exclaimed. "In my whole life, I have never drink this stuff. You try to poison me with this."

"Calm down, I'll get you something else."

Dell tried again and prepared hot chocolate for Rita, hoping that would be more acceptable to the South American, and more soothing than Colombian coffee.

After the women became calmer and ready to return to their beds, Dell refused to leave.

"I'll sleep here in the den—or your sitting room, Cindi. Then we'll all feel better."

"The den will be fine," Cindi quickly insisted. "You'll be close to the back stairway for Rita's protection and you will be close enough to me as well. The den is the best place for you."

Dell could tell from her words that she feared his nearness.

The rest of the night passed quietly, and the next morning after breakfast, Dell walked back to the pool house. His mind as fuzzy as if he'd drunk too much champagne, he knew his hang-over stemmed from lack of sleep and the aftermath of fear for Cindi's safety. As agonizing as one caused by drinking sparkling wine, it made his head pound with each footstep.

Tai, retrieved from Cindi's sitting room where the animal had insisted on sleeping, followed his master with an equally careful step. His lugubrious face looked more solemn and subdued than usual. Once back at the pool house, the dog flopped down on the patio, too tired to go farther. Dell knew his dog's uneasiness last night had brought him over to the house in time to hear the panther scream. In time to comfort and help Cindi—and Rita.

After a quick shower and change of clothes, Dell groped around in the scattered piles for his journal.

"Really strange things have been happening around here. Mr. Jim's partner showed up the day after Cindi came. He and a Colombian woman he brought with him are teamed up somehow. The other day, I overheard them talking and plotting together.

"This same guy, Cliff Aymond, keeps showing up and bringing Cindi news about her pa. The first time he came, he said Mr. Jim was alive and in prison. Now he says the people who have Mr. Jim will release him for a ransom of $200,000. He also told Cindi that Miss Flowers has disappeared as well. I'm afraid the fellow is a scoundrel and the truth is not in him.

"Last night there was a big commotion over at Magnolia House again. Cindi heard a girl's voice crying and calling. She got up but saw nothing. Rita heard something too, but she claimed what she heard was not a woman. She said she heard 'el tigre' or some such creature scream. I heard the scream and I think she's right.

"Ravin' Rita sure looks different when she's not in the kitchen. There she always wears her hair in a tight braided do, but she wears it down at night. What a hot tamale!"

After he finished with his journal, Dell went out on his brick patio to join Tai. The dog shifted his body and head as Dell came out, but refused to get up.

"Too tired to even move, huh?" Dell taunted Tai who just looked at him and yawned, his face the perfect picture of worry and fear. "Some watch dog you are."

But when Tai assumed an offended expression, Dell began to praise him. "Yes you are, old boy. You're truly a lion dog, Tai. You woke me up last night and brought me over to the big house. You have the courage of the lion in your heart. I know you hate to even go inside

Magnolia House, yet last night you slept in Cindi's sitting room to keep her safe." Dell stooped to pet his canine friend as he whispered these words to the dog. Tai seemed to accept them as his just due and his expression turned to satisfaction.

Today, the stormy night had given way to perfect weather. The temperature had warmed, but a cooling fresh breeze blew from the south. The only signs remaining of the storm were puddles on the uneven bricks of the patio, plus debris on the grounds.

Dell stretched carefully to limber up for his morning exercises. Sleeping over at the main house on the couch had left him with more kinks to work out than usual. He performed his morning routine, carefully avoiding the wet patches with his bare feet. His concentration was lacking and he failed to give close attention to the moves he usually managed with unconscious grace. He wound up the exercises frustrated and disgusted with his lack of discipline, but at least feeling much less pain.

"Might as well get to work picking this mess up," he said to Tai.

The usually well-kept grounds were littered with leaves torn from the magnolia trees and branches ripped from the oaks and pines during the melee of wind and rain. Dell's pride would not allow them to remain that way. He began cleaning them up and looking for any real damage caused by the storm. As he picked up the fallen limbs and magnolia leaves, he also checked the barbed wire fence that ran around the property. The physical labor restored him and kept thoughts of Cindi at bay.

An open spot in the fencing on the east side of the property drew his attention. It looked as if someone had separated the wires and crawled through. Like the doors to the house, there was no alarm system on the fence. Most of the locals gave the place a wide berth anyway due to the ghost tales circulating about it.

The property on the other side of the fence belonged to Samantha Carver and her husband Jeff. Cordelia's parents. It was familiar ground though forbidden to him now. Dell slipped silently through the brush looking for some sign of the identity of the person who had breached the fence.

A murmur of low voices caused him to pull himself up onto a low-hanging oak limb. There he flattened himself out on the rough bark.

As he waited there, Rita and Cliff strolled into view. Cliff's low-pitched voice carried better than Rita's shrill tones which at first were an unintelligible questioning babble. Dell could hear Cliff explaining why he hadn't come to Rita's room last night though, so he surmised what she had been asking.

"Jeff and I had to get ready for tonight's shipment, honey. I was too tired when we got through," Cliff was saying.

"I wish you had been there to see '*el tigre*.'"

The two had halted beneath Dell's tree and he could hear her clearly now.

"I wouldn't have been able to see this animal even if I'd been there," Cliff objected. "I'd have had to stay hidden in your room anyway. I'm sure it probably was nothing but Dell's stupid dog."

"You could peek out," Rita argued. "And this thing is too big for a dog. It is '*el tigre*' come for me—to get me for my sins. That ghost voice scare me too. I needed you, Cliff."

"I wish I could have been there for you," Cliff said.

Dell wondered if Rita heard the ironic, insincere tone in Cliff's voice. If not, the guy really had her fooled.

"When will I be able to leave Magnolia House?" Rita asked next. "I don't like staying around there now I know it is haunted."

"You know better than that. It's not haunted. Half the things that have happened, you made happen. Get a grip, Rita."

Cliff's voice sounded sharp now, and Rita began to cry.

"I do not like this Magnolia House. It is truly haunted. The things I do to scare Cindi are as nothing beside the real haunts that live there."

"It will be all right," Cliff said and drew Rita into his arms and began to kiss her.

Dell could hardly keep himself from twisting away in disgust as he watched from the branch above them.

After a few more affectionate sounding whispers between the two, Cliff gave Rita's backside a pat and sent her off down the path toward Miss Flowers' property. Once Rita was out of sight, Cliff retreated the other way.

Dell slipped soundlessly from the tree and followed Cliff. He was sure Cliff was bound for Jeff Carver's business site and he meant to try to discover something about this shipment Cliff had mentioned.

CHAPTER 8

Breakfast for Cindi had been a tense affair of *chocolate santaferena* and toast. Then Dell left for his own house, with no time for amusing chit-chat and not a glance in Cindi's direction. She was too worn out from her night of interrupted sleep to deal with him anyway, so she retired to her room to bathe and rest awhile.

After her rest, she walked to the mailbox down at the end of the driveway. She found a letter from a friend who was her former piano teacher in Lake Charles. She eagerly tore it open and read it. The letter gave her a surge of excitement. The teacher and her son, Lee, wanted to come for a visit. Cindi's spirits lifted at the thought of congenial company—and more people—in the house.

Back at the house, she searched for Rita, hoping to find out if the woman felt up to cooking for company. She roamed through the downstairs unable to call out Rita's name because her healing throat would not allow it. She even made a fruitless trip to Rita's room, knocking on the door and getting no response.

At loose ends, she spent some time in the flowery atrium aimlessly searching for any clue to the shadowy figure that often appeared there. Then Cindi decided to go back upstairs to Rita's room, even though she knew she really should respect the South American woman's privacy. She felt she must take this chance to search there.

She found the room neat enough. The only things out of place in an otherwise neat room was the gaudy red nightwear Rita had worn the night before which had been thrown carelessly on the bed. Then Cindi noticed that scent again. The same smell that bugged her the night Rita had talked with her after the midnight concert permeated the woman's bedroom. Stuck in Cindi's mind as securely as an aggravating grass burr was the nagging certainty she should be able to name the familiar fragrance.

She concluded her unrewarding search, left the room and started down the stairs. Cindi slipped and fell flat on her backside at the landing. One hand landed hard against the first riser. Her sensitive fingertips felt a slight offset there.

Curiously she traced the outline of the riser as she lay there catching her breath and recovering from the shock of the fall. Finally Cindi flipped over to look. Nothing seemed amiss, but as she ran her fingers over the smooth wood, she touched a recessed catch. The whole front of the step fell forward exposing a dark cubbyhole. She could not resist reaching in. Her hand encountered a bumpy pouch which, as she pulled it out, she found curiously heavy for its small size.

Cautiously, Cindi pushed the front of the step back in. It fit tightly, looked perfectly the same as the others. Then she bent an inquiring glance at the mysterious pouch.

One glance was all she got.

"*Senorita?* Miss Cindi? Where are you?"

"Rats," Cindi muttered under her breath as Rita's shrill voice interrupted her examination of the fascinating pouch. "I've been looking for her and now when I want some privacy she shows up." Cindi stuffed her find through the placket of her shirt and into her bra.

"Rita?" Cindi answered as loudly as she could. "Is that you? Here I am—on the stairs."

"What happen? Did you fall? Are you hurt?" Rita asked as she climbed the stairs and helped Cindi up from the floor.

"I slipped coming downstairs, but I'm not hurt—except for my pride. I was looking for you. I thought you might be in your room," Cindi said defensively, afraid Rita might guess she'd been searching her room. "I wanted to call, but all I could manage was a little squeak. Where were you?"

As she demanded to know Rita's whereabouts, a memory of where she'd smelled the scent the woman wore overwhelmed her. She remembered being in a car with Cliff. He was taking her home to her mother, and explaining why he would not marry her. The fragrance had been strong in the car. It was Cliff's favorite cologne, an expensive men's fragrance.

During that car ride, as she'd discovered that Cliff had been toying with her affections, the odor turned cloying and repulsive in Cindi's nostrils. Strange that Rita should choose to wear a man's fragrance. As her mind struggled with the memory, Cindi heard Rita answer.

"I just go for a walk. All my work is done. I need to get out of this haunted place sometime."

Cindi found Rita's manner sly and defensive, so she answered quickly, "I'm not complaining. I understand perfectly. I was looking for you to tell you we will have guests this weekend. That is, if you don't mind."

"Guests? What kind of people would want to come to such a place as this?'

"Friends of mine who want to see me, I guess." The words left Cindi's mouth before she gave them a thought. "Sorry," she apologized. "I mean, these are old friends of mine, my former piano teacher and her son."

"Who would bring a little boy here?" Rita raved in an argumentative tone and a shrug of her shoulders in dismissal of Cindi's friend's *loco* behavior.

"Her son isn't a little boy. He's my age." Cindi laughed. "My friends live here in Louisiana and I haven't seen them since I left for school in California. They know there are strange things happening here and they still want to come. I wrote them about the house when I first got here."

"They know about *el tigre*?"

"No," Cindi had to admit. That was one ghost story she hadn't told them. "I've only told them about the midnight concert, that's all." *And about someone going through my things, but that's all I'm going to share with you, since you're probably the one responsible for that.*

"Maybe if they know about him they would not want to come," Rita insisted, not sounding too happy at the thought of more people to cook for and clean up after.

"Him? Oh, you mean this tiger you claim you heard. I'll tell them what happened last night when I call to tell them they can come," Cindi said. "I know I'll feel safer with more people in the house. Won't you?"

"Maybe you are right about that, *senorita*," Rita agreed. "Safety in *grande numeros,* I guess. How many rooms should I get ready?"

"Only two," Cindi answered with a smile. "Our guests will be Marie Guidroz and her son, Lee. Miss Marie was my first piano teacher. And Lee and I started school together. Thanks for being agreeable, Rita."

Cindi and Rita headed to the kitchen to check supplies and plan menus. The moment they got there, Cindi called the Guidrozes to let them know they were welcome.

Then she returned to the kitchen to help Rita plan the menus and decide what supplies might be needed.

Now and then a twinge of discomfort reminded her of the lumpy pouch still secreted in her bra. Each time this happened, she felt a surge of curiosity.

Just as Cindi finished and could retire to her room to examine her find, she heard a car pull up at the front of the house.

"I wonder who could be dropping by this morning," Cindi remarked. "I'm not expecting anyone."

"Me neither," Rita said, adding in a whining tone. "Until the weekend, when your friends come." Cindi went to the door to find Samantha Carver waiting there. Cindi forced herself to smile and greet the woman nicely.

"I received a book yesterday from the main library that I think you might like to take a look at," the librarian said after returning Cindi's greeting. "It's a collection of editorials and tales from a newspaper once published here in Caddo Parish. Some of them date back to the thirties and forties. Knowing you were interested in the history of this part of the country, I just brought it on out to you. I'm on my lunch break."

"You've certainly put yourself out to do me a service," Cindi said. "This is the kind of Southern hospitality I remember from my younger days when I was growing up in the south part of the state."

"Oh, it was no bother really. I'm on my way home. I live a mile farther up the road," Samantha responded.

"You're our nearest neighbor then," Cindi remarked. "For some reason I assumed you lived in town. Stop by anytime."

As Cindi mouthed these polite phrases she was thinking, no wonder Dell had his wreck so near here. He must have been taking Cordelia home when it happened. But why hasn't he mentioned that the Carvers are our neighbors? In fact, I distinctly remember him saying we didn't have any close neighbors.

"I really must get on to the house, or I won't have time for a sandwich," Cordelia's mother was saying as Cindi pulled herself back to their conversation.

"Perhaps you'd like to come by Saturday night. Some friends of mine from south Louisiana are coming for a visit," Cindi said. "I'd like for you to stop by and meet them. Come for dessert and coffee about eight o'clock or so. It'll be casual dress, so just wear what's comfortable. Oh, and bring your husband." *I probably shouldn't be so nosy, but maybe if they come I can find out more about Cordelia.*

Samantha agreed to stop by on Saturday then left for home.

Cindi decided to double-check the food in the refrigerator. While she was in the kitchen, Dell entered the house through the den. Cindi asked him if he could make a trip to town.

"We need more milk and bread," Cindi said. "And where do you get those eggs?"

"The eggs come from a lady in town who keeps chickens. I'll be glad to pick up anything you need," Dell answered. "Just be sure all the doors are locked. I think someone's been trespassing on the grounds." He told her about the telltale gap he'd found in the fence.

"I promise to lock up carefully," Cindi promised.

"I will go with Dell," Rita said, as she bustled back into the kitchen. "I want to pick out some special things just for our guests."

As Dell and Rita left, Cindi carefully locked all the doors. She went into her rooms and made sure every door to the master suite was locked there as well. She closed every drape before pulling out the pouch for examination.

No one but a nosy helicopter pilot hovering over the skylight would be able to catch a glimpse now, she thought.

She laid the small bag on the bedside table and inspected it. The maroon velvet pouch, damp with her perspiration and warm to the touch from the heat of her body, fascinated her.

She stared at it, hesitating to release its twisted closure. Finally she loosened the drawstring and turned the pouch upside down over the bed. As what looked like a treasure of unset, deep green stones poured out; she gasped and blinked her eyes. *Emeralds—they look like emeralds.*

Though Cindi was no expert, the clarity and deep color of the stones convinced her they were authentic and of great value. This must be what Rita had been searching for. She picked some up in her cupped palms.

She imagined a mystical power emanating from them. They assuredly were worth a king's ransom or, even more importantly to Cindi, Jim Lynn's ransom. She wished they were hers and that she knew how to turn them into cash. She slowly spread her fingers, admiring the fiery gleam of the gems as they fell through.

Mesmerized by the glow and sensual feel of the stones, Cindi only gradually became aware of a persistent tapping sound.

The tapping came from the patio off the master suite.

Believing herself to be alone at the house, the sound of someone knocking at her door made her heart pound in fear.

She scooped up the stones and replaced them in the pouch. No better hiding place than the first one she'd stashed them in occurred to her. With a muffled oath, she replaced the pouch in her bra.

She started toward the patio door, not sure what to do. She knew only too well that she was completely alone and vulnerable. Making a tiny peephole in the drapes, she peered out. The person knocking was Cliff, patiently standing before the glass door.

His gaze directed at the creamy flowered magnolias circling the house, his face wore a weary cast. Cindi's fears for her father resurfaced. In her heart she was sure Cliff would not brave her anger if he were not the bearer of the very best or the very worst news of all. Her heart lurched with a painful bump as she threw open the door.

"Cliff, please tell me why you're here?" she cried. "Have you been able to negotiate with my father's captors?"

"Oh Cindi, Cindi love. I'm afraid I have very bad news," Cliff answered. "I needed to be with you when I told you."

Stunned, Cindi allowed him to enter the sitting room and grasp her upper arms. His hold punishing and anything but gentle, he pulled her toward him.

"I've never found anyone else like you," Cliff murmured huskily. "You know I love you." His piercing blue eyes shone with a fanatical gleam.

To Cindi, they held no true desire or tenderness. In their depths she saw only a desperate need to convince her of his overwhelming passion for her. Such a ludicrous, overdone attempt—she almost laughed in his face.

"If you think I believe that, you've got mush for brains. You've gone off the deep end," Cindi responded as she rejected his bogus emotion and struggled to get out of his embrace. "Remember I'm not a naive teenager anymore. Just come out with this news of my father you claim to have. And take your hands off me."

Her brave words did not convince Cliff to let go of her. As the man continued to hold her arms, Cindi kicked him sharply in the shin to gain his attention.

"Let me go," she demanded and continued to struggle to free herself. "What about my father? Any news?"

Cliff released her, then responded, "That's what I've come to tell you. I'm afraid your father is dead. He's been murdered."

His callous words made Cindi wild with grief.

Somewhere far off, she could hear a woman keening in a high, mindless tone. She could not associate the sound with herself. She felt as if she were somewhere far above the room looking down at the woman who stood close by Cliff's side. Then once again she felt herself begin a helpless downward spiral as the floor tilted up to meet her.

In her last moment of consciousness, she heard Dell's voice calling her name and an insistent pounding on her bedroom door.

When she came to her senses she found herself in Dell's arms with no sign of Cliff .

"Where's Cliff?" she demanded. "He must tell me it's a lie. My father can't be dead. Make him say he lied."

The look in Dell's eyes confused her. What was wrong? Could what Cliff had said be true? Once again she began to plead with Dell to reveal Cliff's whereabouts.

"Cindi, Cliff is nowhere around," Dell said patiently. "I haven't seen him. You ran him off yesterday. You must be having delusions or something. When I unlocked your door, you were lying on the floor. What's wrong?" He lifted her tenderly and carried her toward a chaise lounge.

Cindi tried to gather her thoughts, but the feel of Dell's sinewy arms as they held her so securely, flustered her. Her disturbed mind slipped into denial of anything else but the safety she felt there. He held her the same comforting, exciting way he had held her in the sanctuary of St. Elisabeth Church. Her mind wanted to stay on these safe emotions.

She pushed away the message Cliff had brought her. Dell had told her Cliff had never been here. Surely he knew what he was talking about. She must have been mistaken. Cliff had never been here, never brought her news of her father's death.

She stirred in Dell's arms and moved closer to him. But as she did, she saw his gaze turn to surprise and accusation as he dropped her unceremoniously onto the quilted surface of the lounge.

"What have you found? Where did you get that?" Dell gasped.

She looked down and saw the small pouch poking from her blouse. "Do you mean this?" she asked as she pulled it from its hiding place. "I found this sack of stones hidden on the stairs this morning. But I could easily have come upon them anytime, or even brought them with me."

"No you didn't. I've seen this pouch before. Those stones are the Delgado emeralds Miss Flowers put away for a nest egg."

Cindi studied his face and saw no guile there. Her held-in breath whooshed out. The sound surprised her. She hadn't even been aware of holding the air in.

"Did you know where they were hidden?" Cindi asked as she replenished the air in her lungs with a deep cleansing breath.

"No," Dell admitted. "I don't think she trusted anyone else with their location. Not even your father. May I?" He took the pouch from her, opened it, and poured the stones into his long, tapering palm where they glowed warmly.

Cindi shrugged as if it made no difference to her. "Go ahead." She could hardly object even though she longed to. The stones weren't hers after all, no matter how much she wished they were.

"Do you know what these are worth?" Dell asked.

"Not really, but I have an idea they must be very valuable. Maybe even valuable enough to provide the money for my father's ransom."

Sudden loud shouting in what sounded like gutter Spanish assaulted their ears. As one, they started toward the sound.

CHAPTER 9

Dell and Cindi hurried toward the sound of the strident Spanish tirade. They moved with hands clasped together. When they first heard the shouting, they'd naturally joined hands.

Now Cindi heard Cliff's voice dueling with Rita's. His sounded distressed and put upon. Rita sounded fiercely annoyed. Since both were speaking Spanish for the most part, Cindi only understood a word here and there. And, she realized with panic, it was often her name that she understood.

The two voices sounded like an operatic duet. Rita's hovered over Cliff's with her shrill, unmusical tone. Cliff's provided a more melodic basso profundo counterpoint.

Even their poses as Dell and Cindi entered the kitchen, and found them, mimicked comic opera. Rita stood over Cliff spouting what sounded like curses at him. She held a heavy iron skillet in a threatening manner. Cliff, half-knelt on the floor on one leg, held up his arms to ward off her attack.

Cindi fought an inappropriate urge to laugh. She refused to let her mouth form a tremulous grin. Her emotions, stretched to the breaking point by all the changes the day had brought, reacted in strange ways. Her expressive face wanted to show all of them.

"Now wait a minute," Dell said in a quiet, commanding voice. "You two can probably be heard all the way to Ida. Rita, put that skillet down. Cliff, get up from the floor."

As Dell took charge, Cindi felt better. His strength soothed her frazzled nerves as he stepped up and disarmed Rita.

Quickly, Cliff scrambled up, composed his face and attempted to present his usual debonair facade.

"Rita has me all wrong," he claimed. "She thinks I'm paying too much attention to Cindi."

Dell agreed with Rita, but he wasn't about to admit it, only asking, "What started all this? What set Rita off?"

Though he'd been addressing Cliff, Rita answered, rattling Spanish and English words like an electronic printer gone mad.

The gist of her speech, as Dell translated freely to Cindi, was something like this.

"I come to find Cliff and he is in Cindi's room. He was bending down to take her in his arms. I see him through her patio door. He see me and come to me. I tell him he must come with me to the kitchen, I have something to show him."

Dell shook his head. "And you couldn't wait to find out why he was with Cindi before you decided to show him the blunt side of your frying pan, I guess. You didn't care that he was trying to pick her up because she'd fainted when he told her about her father's death." Dell's patience had run out and his own temper rose to the same pitch of Rita's and Cliff's.

"Why did you go off and leave her on the floor?" Dell asked as he turned toward the other man. Rage filled him and threatened to overflow into violence.

"I had to see what Rita was talking about," Cliff defended himself.

"Why didn't you tell me Mr. Jim is dead?" Rita demanded and broke into a rapid volley of Spanish curses once more.

Cliff held up his hands. "Enough, Rita. Quiet down. You didn't give me a chance to tell you."

"*Madre Dios*! So Mr. Jim is dead. I cannot believe it. I am sorry, *senorita*," Rita declared, her voice still loud but falling in volume now. "You must not try to steal my man, though. Cliff belongs to me. He is mine. We are together almost every night."

Cindi stared at the Spanish woman, loathing the smug smile that curved her lips. Though Rita was welcome to Cliff if she wanted him, her arrogant smile reminded Cindi of the taunting smile on Consuelo's painted face. The curious resemblance between the two women bothered her. They might share more similarities than a cruel smile.

"Just now Cliff tell me you are his 'one and only love,'" Rita said next. "He say he still love you and want you back. I could kill him for that."

Dell reached for the heavy skillet he had placed on the table, scooting it out of Rita's grasp.

"You damn near did kill me," Cliff put in. "You were trying to brain me with that thing. That's why I was down on the floor. I sure wasn't trying to propose. I tripped trying to get away from you."

"Is it really true about my father?" Cindi asked in a very small, lost-sounding voice. She drew a deep breath and struggled not to cry. She ignored Rita's and Cliff's last words.

"I'm sorry, Cindi. That's the last thing I heard from his captors," Cliff said in a gentler voice. "They called me on my car phone. They claimed he tried to escape and they shot him as he was boarding a plane out of the country."

"Nothing more than that?" questioned Cindi with tears in her eyes. "Where is his body? Will they ship his body to me?"

"I think it was a seaplane, and his body fell into the water," Cliff explained uneasily. "It wasn't recovered."

"How very convenient—for them. That way they don't have to come up with any evidence that he is dead. If he isn't, they can keep him in their filthy prison forever and we will never know any different." Cindi ended her bitter words with a long sigh.

As she regained her breath, she continued. "All this time I've been praying I wouldn't be left without at least one parent. Here at Magnolia House, I've felt close to father—as if I've gotten him back at last. I don't know if I can stand it now, if he's never coming back."

Cindi burst into hard sobs and Dell cradled her gently in his arms.

"You two act as if Cindi is the only one who ever lost her parents. You are spoiled, soft *Norte Americains* who have never had to know what it is to have your whole family killed by the government," Rita said. "That's what happened to mine."

She looked directly at Dell as she poured forth these venomous thoughts, but her words bit into Cindi's heart. Seeking to escape them, Cindi shrank closer to Dell.

"Why do you hate me so?" she whispered to Rita as she lifted her head to stare at the woman from perplexed, tear-filled eyes. "I've always tried to treat you with kindness."

"Kindness? Is kindness to take my man? Cliff say he want you. He say Dell don't deserve you. I get my skillet to punish him. Maybe I should punish you instead."

"Come on, Rita, calm down," Cliff urged. "That's not exactly what

I said."

"Shut up, Cliff," Rita screamed. "You can't fool me. You want Cindi."

Cindi could tell Rita wasn't about to calm down. Cliff's sexual magnetism wasn't working its usual magic. Rita wasn't buying Cliff's excuses this time.

"Cliff, I think you'd better leave for now," Dell said as he sheltered Cindi in his arms. "Rita has cleaning and lots of other preparations to make. Cindi is expecting company this weekend. Go away and don't come back unless you really have some news. Don't be sneaking back to see Rita either. If you need to see her that much, take her with you now."

"That won't be necessary," Cliff answered, his suave manner once more in place. "Rita needs time to think. I've got things to do as well. Most importantly, I've a trip to make to Baton Rouge to qualify for the governor's race."

"Humph," Cindi sniffed. "Louisiana politics never cease to amaze me. Hit the road—you need to get a start to wherever it is you're really headed."

Cliff left with a disgruntled look on his face. Dell left saying he needed to mow the grass. Cindi and Rita cleaned the kitchen in silence, both working with feverish energy. Needing to deal with the sadness that settled over her at the thought of her father's death, Cindi welcomed the hard work necessary to get the house ready for her friends arrival. She supposed Rita was working off her anger at Cliff. The atmosphere around Magnolia house began to calm down.

Once the kitchen was clean and straight again, Cindi zipped through the bottom floor putting things in order, dusting and running the vacuum. The monotonous physical work calmed her as it always did. At Cindi's suggestion, Rita went upstairs to put fresh linen on the beds.

Cindi made an inventory of serving pieces available for the informal dessert party she planned for Saturday night. She then engaged in a mindless task that always soothed her nerves best of all, polishing silver. She found an ornate coffee service in the dining area china cabinet. It would be perfect for some of Rita's strong Colombian coffee.

She had just finished bringing the set to a satisfying gloss when Dell came through the French doors from the rear deck.

"As soon as you finish that job, would you like to come over to the pool house to see my paintings?" he asked with a teasing glint in his eye.

Cindi rewarded him with a tiny smile. "If you're trying to cheer me up by using that corny old line, it's working. I'm near enough through. We can go on over now."

"Where's Rita?" Dell asked as he and Cindi made their way to his place.

"I sent her upstairs to make beds and clean bathrooms. I couldn't stand having her near me."

"That's good," Dell approved. "I wanted to tell you that I overheard her and Cliff talking earlier today in the woods. Just like yesterday when I heard them as Cliff was on his way out."

"So what did you hear?"

"This morning they were talking about what happened last night. Also doing a lot of hugging and kissing and talking about tonight and some kind of shipment that was coming in. I'm not sure what the shipment is, but I think I know where it's coming in—over at Jeff Carver's helicopter place."

"Jeff's helicopter place? Where is that?"

"The Carver Helicopter Service in on their property, and not far from here."

"Well, according to what Rita told me, if it's coming from Colombia, I guess it could be almost anything from drugs to emeralds."

"Right. Rita also went on and on about '*el tigre*.' She seemed really scared so I don't think she had anything to do with last night's scare. Cliff had to talk fast to persuade her to stay here at Magnolia House. He told her to keep looking for whatever's hidden here."

"I suppose the emeralds I happened to find are what they've been looking for," Cindi said.

"We'll have to find a good place to put those things," Dell said. "I've still got them. Do you have any idea where we can hide them?"

"I guess you better give them to me. There must be a good place for them in Consuelo's room. I'll think of something."

The small, heavy pouch changed hands. Cindi turned away to slip it back into her bra just as they reached Dell's room. There, Cindi found just being in his intimate, private space brought her pain. She felt as if she had found a true home, but wouldn't be asked to stay. When her gaze found her little girl portrait, half-finished, her eyes widened in surprise. She walked over to the easel and examined it.

"That's me," she said unnecessarily. "What a forlorn little twerp I was. How could you know how I looked back then?" A small frown marred her forehead as she spoke.

She turned to him to find him studying her with an amused air. "How long have you been working on this?"

"Did anyone ever tell you that you ask too many questions? Or that you should never play poker?" Dell asked, turning the tables on her.

"No and no," Cindi answered. "Now answer my questions."

Dell obliged with a smile. "I'll just bet they didn't. Anyway, your pa asked me to do this for him before he went to Colombia. He gave me your photograph to work from. He said it might give him back his little girl just as he remembered you when he had to leave. No wonder you looked forlorn."

As Dell finished his amazingly long speech, his second of the day, Cindi covered her telltale face with her hands. She glanced at the photograph Dell pointed out as his model. Then, she bent over slightly and breathed deeply to avoid crying.

"He did care. He did miss me," she gasped on the verge of tears.

Dell could stand it no longer. He gathered her into his arms and comforted her by stroking her beautiful hair. "You must know your pa loved you very much. Don't ever doubt that. He would never have left you if there had been any way he could have stayed with your mother," he said. All the while he spoke, he shook his head in denial of any other explanation of Cindi's father's separation from her and her mother. "For your own sake, please forgive him for what he did."

"Oh, Dell, how could you know that I've always held his leaving against him? How could you know I've always felt he abandoned me to my foolish, childish mother?"

"Your face shows me every emotion you feel. You can hide nothing from me, dearest."

"Well you constantly amaze me," Cindi said. She wanted to kiss him and snuggle closer in his arms, but she broke free and walked around the room looking at all the paintings there. She kept her silence as she examined them all.

Many were landscapes of nearby places. Poignant ones of St. Elisabeth Baptist Church and desolate Spoonful Bar were among them. The magnolia trees with their creamy blooms and one stunning one of Magnolia House. At last she gave her judgment.

"In my opinion, my father did right to encourage you, Dell. These are wonderful. Have you ever thought of having a one man show?"

"There you go with the questions again. I'll reserve my answer to that till later. Now there is something you could help me with. Ever since you came, I've wanted to paint you as you are now, all grown up. Please Cindi, say you will sit for me."

"I might, but why would you want to paint me?"

"It would please me very much," he answered.

* * *

Later when Cindi decided to do some serious sunbathing on the private patio off the master suite, Tai joined her. She settled on a chaise lounge, Tai jumped up on the other one. The two lay in contented companionship. Today the dog showed no signs of the nervousness that had been evident when he spent the night in Cindi's sitting room.

He's either getting used to being over here at the big house or else "el tigre" is nowhere around.

Scratching the dog's head and observing his complete relaxation, Cindi decided she was right. Tai's tongue lolled from his mouth as he basked in the sun's rays, and the comfort of her undivided attention. In turn, she basked in the sun determined to keep her California tan. She wore a scanty pink bikini she dared not appear in around Dell. A bikini that fit a little less snugly than the last time she wore it, but still revealed too much of her now sleeker, svelter curves. Close at hand was a cover-up to don at the first sound of anyone's approach. She'd pushed up her long hair under a California Angels baseball cap, pulled low to shade her face.

Dell had retreated to his little house to paint after he finished mowing the lawn. He'd told her he wanted to finish her childhood portrait so he could start the one he really wanted to do. She didn't expect him to come near the big house.

Feeling well done on the front, Cindi turned over so her back could catch some rays. "Tai," she addressed the dog, and reached over to fondle his ears, "you must help me make sense of the things that have been happening around here. And of your master. After all, you know Dell better than most."

Tai gave a short snuffle that sounded encouraging to Cindi. She didn't feel odd talking to the dog. In her lonely, growing-up years, she'd often conversed with her mother's Siamese cats. She'd always found talks with them brought remarkable insights into problems. Perhaps a chat with Tai might do the same.

After all, animals with their origin in the Orient should have the wisdom of Confucius in their brain.

At that slightly goofy thought, Cindi almost giggled aloud. Better not, she cautioned herself. Talking to Tai is one thing. Laughing with him might mean she was nuts.

Tai cocked his head inquiringly at that moment as if he wanted to be privy to her every thought. Cindi obliged by telling him how much she thought of his master. She admitted at first she wondered at Consuelo trusting him to care for the huge estate by himself. And never once calling to check on the upkeep and security. She finished by deeming Dell strong as Rita's Colombian coffee, and completely worthy of Consuelo's trust.

Her eyes softened momentarily as she thought of Dell who always made her feel safe and comforted by his presence. "But, Tai, even though I can see how she could trust Dell, why didn't she ever call to welcome me or inquire how things were in the house? Where is she?"

Tai gave an inquisitive "woof" and waggled his hindquarters and curly tail. Cindi relaxed even more and let her hand drop from the petting position. She reached back to untie her top, then flipped back over to expose her front side to the sun's rays just a little more. Soon she went fast asleep. Her dreams once again were of Dell.

As she slept, Dell entered the walled patio. Slipping in on bare feet, he came to stand over her. Her semi-nude beauty awed him. Her skin was a light honey tone, turning pink now on her bared breasts. He couldn't tear his eyes away from the captivating sight of those twin globes. Tipped with rosy circles centering her tantalizing nipples, her tawny breasts were perfection. Their curves tapering in to her ridiculously tiny waist then flaring out at her lush hips covered only by the brief bikini bottom. Her slender legs stretched out to the sun. The bulk of her pale hair was twisted up under the baseball cap, but loose tendrils escaped to wave gently around her luminous face. He longed to smooth them back. He longed to kiss her parted lips.

Caressing her fully with his gaze, he longed to drop down and bury his head against her breasts. He hungered to take her delicate, pale pink nipples one by one pulling those tight budded tips into his mouth to suckle.

He left as silently as he had come. He never touched her. He returned to his own place, and from memory began to sketch what he had seen as she and the dog slept. Working in a haze of creative energy, he put what he had seen down on paper. Then he placed a fresh canvas on the easel and began to block out an oil of her just that way.

He would remind her she'd promised to pose for him as soon as her friends had come and gone. He would do another portrait of her, a more formal one. That way nothing could ever take her from him. She would always be his.

CHAPTER 10

No off-key singing, no banging pots, no greeting at all came from Rita the next morning. The usually vibrant woman merely continued fussing with the coffeepot and making a production of lifting the cheese toast from the oven when Cindi entered the kitchen. She was far from noisy, and anything but raving—completely out of character.

No ghostly visits or unusual sounds had marred Cindi's sleep either. She'd been sad when she fell asleep thinking perhaps Cliff had given her the truth about her father. Now after a good night's rest, she felt more hopeful. More sure he'd been lying. She wanted to talk to Rita. How could she get Rita started?

"I slept really well last night," she began. "How about you?"

Rita did not reply.

"Oh good, I'm glad you fixed a light breakfast," Cindi observed next.

Rita only shrugged.

Cindi helped herself to the cheese toast and poured herself a glass of orange juice. "Last night was so peaceful. I hope you slept as well as I did," she said.

Rita remained mute. Her only reply another noncommittal shrug. The room resonated with silence. Rita seated herself at the table with a steaming cup of coffee. She gazed into the garden room as if Cindi were nowhere around.

Frustrated, Cindi fumed. She hoped to get some clues from Rita about her relationship with Cliff, and her real reason for being at

Magnolia House. She wanted to know about the mysterious final shipment due at Carver's airstrip last night. Was there any way to get Rita to drop a clue?

Cindi couldn't stand it. She tried to think of something else to say. She had to break the tension between them. Making a fresh start, she began again.

"What's wrong, Rita? I'm just trying to be civil." Cindi walked over and poured herself more coffee. She brought the pot over to warm up Rita's cup. "If we can't be friends, can't we at least engage in polite conversation? Please don't let Cliff cause us to disagree."

Rita continued to stare at the atrium, though she did take a sip of her freshened coffee.

"Come on, Rita. I swear I have no interest in Cliff. In fact, I'm glad he's fond of you." Cindi sat next to Rita, and by force of will tried to draw the woman's gaze to her instead of the flowers. "Do you think you and I can start over?"

A truculent frown appeared on Rita's face. Then she began to cry instead of spouting the angry words Cindi was expecting.

"It's not you, *senorita*," she said as she wept noisily. "I am just afraid Cliff will get tired of me. Sometimes he is not good to me, but you have always been good to me just like Mr. Jim."

"I've just treated you like I'd want to be treated myself," Cindi said. "Believe me, I haven't been particularly kind or good. As for Cliff, he can be a heel at times. I should know. He's the one who ended things between us years ago. You don't have to worry about me as competition. I think he's just pretending to want me to make you jealous. He threw me over, and I was crushed at first, but I got over that. I care nothing for him now." The long speech taxed Cindi's voice. She ended the words in a tiny squeak, and patted Rita's hand for reassurance.

"If that is so, it work," Rita replied and gave a small, watery smile. "It work. I'm jealous. Me and Cliff, *por Dios* permit, God willing…maybe I keep him, maybe not. Maybe he, how you say, throw me over, too. Maybe he is too big a heel, is that how you say?"

"You said it just right."

"If Cliff do that, I would have to go back to Colombia. I have no visa, no permit to be here if I do not marry an American citizen. Colombia is my home, but things are not always so good there. The government killed my parents. I have no family to go back to. Everyone in my family is dead or in prison. I have nothing back there in my country."

Cindi wondered why Rita had suddenly decided to confide in her. She wondered if the story about her family was true. "I'm sorry, Rita," she said, deciding to take the story at face value. "You can always stay on here."

"You would hide me from the officials? Thank you, *senorita.* You and me, maybe we can be friends now?"

Rita's offer of friendship touched Cindi. She decided to reassure the woman as much as she could, though she would never do anything illegal. "All right, friend." She offered her hand to Rita.

"Making peace, girls?" Dell queried as he entered the kitchen in time to hear their last exchange. He gave Cindi's pale hair an absentminded tousle as he leaned over to grab a piece of toast. "It'll make for a better, calmer visit for Cindi's friends that way."

"I'm glad you approve." Cindi smiled and smoothed her hair in a self-conscious motion. She wondered if he'd overheard Rita's words about Cliff. "I can't wait to show Miss Marie and Lee how beautiful Magnolia House is. I wouldn't want anything to spoil their visit."

She left Dell and Rita in the kitchen preparing lunch while she put the finishing touches on the house. Dell's job was to carve a small watermelon into a basket to be filled with melon balls, peach slices, orange sections and sugar-frosted grapes. He promised to bring all his artistic flair to bear on the project.

As the time for her guests' expected arrival neared, Cindi went out to plunder the magnolia trees of blossoms. She filled the house with arrangements of the creamy blooms including the guest rooms where Lee and Marie would be sleeping. The whole place redolent with pleasant, lemony fragrance, she sat down at the piano to play all her favorite pieces of music as she waited. Many of the tunes she played were ones she first learned under Miss Marie's instruction.

Around noon, Miss Marie and Lee arrived. Cindi greeted them with joy. She hugged her teacher then stepped back to look at her, all the while holding the lady's small, competent hands.

"Goodness, child, you act as if you think I might just disappear," Miss Marie admonished.

"It's just so great to see you. You're just the same, Miss Marie," Cindi said as she took in the older woman's small delicate frame, crisp gray curls and still sparkling green eyes. The teacher's soft print dress might have been one she'd worn in Cindi's childhood. Cindi had never seen Miss Marie wear slacks or jeans, only print dresses made in the same simple style. Her dresses only differed in weight—lighter cotton voile in the broiling summertime to heavier cotton broadcloth during the mild Southern winters.

"And I remember that violet cologne you're wearing. It reminds me of long ago in Lake Charles," she added as she caught the light flowery scent of violets that since her earliest memory had always surrounded her teacher.

"Thanks for letting us come," Miss Marie answered. "As for you, you're looking better than you ever did back then. Happier. Yes, that's it, happier."

Cindi smiled. "I was a solemn, solitary little thing, wasn't I?"

Her teacher laughed. "You're bigger now."

"Bigger than you at last." Cindi laughed again, and held up her spread fingers. "Let's measure."

Miss Marie obliged. She was a tiny woman, just nine inches over four feet tall.

"I always wondered how you brought such powerful music from any keyboard you touched. That fact always fascinated me," Cindi confided.

Lee entered the house just then. He and Dell brought in the baggage.

"Your hands aren't very big either. They will never be as large as mine," he said. "But they're much prettier." Lee's deep voice growled interest as his dark brown eyes glowed. He reached for Cindi's other hand, which still held on to Miss Marie's. "How do you keep the guys away? You must have had at least a hundred offers of marriage by now. If I remember right, you started out mighty early getting your first one."

Cindi flushed, then laughed. "I'm afraid no one wants me. At least not enough to offer marriage," she said. "Or maybe I'm just too leery of those who might treat me as Cliff did."

"You'd never have to worry about me treating you that way," Lee promised.

"Oh be serious. You're my buddy and always will be. We've been through too much to ever be more than friends. I'll bet you've tons of women crazy over you anyway."

She chanced a peek at Dell's face, anxious to see if he seemed upset at Lee's flirting. His noncommittal look told her nothing. She introduced him as her father's protege and Consuelo's caretaker. He and Lee took the baggage upstairs giving Cindi a chance to speak privately to her teacher.

"I've got to talk to you about Dell," she confided to Miss Marie.

"Of course we'll talk, dear, about anything and everything you'd like to bring up. I also want to hear all about your mother's last days and your own troubles with your throat. I'm sorry we were not able to come to you in California then."

"I truly appreciate that thought. Here at Magnolia House, I've found just about the perfect place to get over all that. When the spirits allow, that is. Now let me show you to your room in this gorgeous, haunted house. Things should be quiet on the upper floor where I've put you two, because most of the haunting goes on in the garden room and living area downstairs."

Cindi went on to describe the latest fright she'd had when the panther appeared. "*El tigre,*" as Rita called the beast.

After the visitors had freshened up, Cindi and Dell showed them the rest of the house and much of the grounds. At the rear deck overlooking pool, Rita stood waiting.

"I am ready to serve lunch," she announced in a glum, unhappy voice. "If you are ready, I'll bring the food right out."

"This is all so beautiful, Cindi," Miss Marie said as she took her place at the glass-topped table.

"I have to apologize for our cook," Cindi said. "Rita is usually a hoot, but she is a little out of sorts today."

"Much quieter, too," Dell added. "Usually she's spouting Spanish non-stop and singing off-key. Maybe it's better this way." He cut his words short as Rita appeared with the food. Cindi jumped up to help Rita.

"I miss your humming as you serve the meals, Rita," Cindi whispered to her as she took Miss Marie's plate. Attempting to bring the woman into the happiness everyone else was enjoying, she added softly. "I miss all your usual comments."

"I am sorry, Miss Cindi. Today I have no happy things to say, so it is better I say nothing."

"Okay. Thanks for fixing this nice meal."

No one but Dell noticed the exchange between Cindi and Rita. He approved their apparent amity, and hoped Rita would soon recover from her unhappiness. As the Colombian woman's usual loud clatter and off-key songs remained unheard and unsung, Dell realized he'd grown accustomed to them and perversely missed them. He wondered if there was something awry. Perhaps something had gone wrong with that mysterious shipment that had been expected last night.

After lunch he invited Lee to join him as he walked the fence. Dell had repaired the spot Rita and Cliff had damaged, and now planned to inspect the whole perimeter for holes daily.

Tai joined them as well, glad of a chance for a romp.

"You've known Cindi quite some time, haven't you?" Dell asked Lee as they started their inspection of the fence.

"My mom took Cindi as a student of piano when Cindi was six. She taught her for ten years or more. I guess you could say I've known her a while. Just about all our lives."

"That's what I thought."

"We've always competed. I always struggled to play piano better, or maybe I should say at least as well, as she does. She's very good. I was jealous of my mother's attention and affection for her as well. It was like sibling rivalry. For a long time I thought of her as a kid sister. They lived next door, and she came over to our house often. And when her lessons were over, she never went home right away. Her own mother was pathetic. She demanded constant attention from Cindi. The only place Cindi could act like a kid was at our place."

"I figured Cindi had to put up with stuff from her mother." Dell spotted a small hole and got out his pliers and a small length of wire to patch it with.

"I've always thought of Cindi as my sister, too. At least that's the way I thought of her until I met her. I claimed her pa as a substitute father, so whenever he talked of Cindi it was like she was my older sister. When I saw her in the flesh…well all I can say is now I've got a bad case of 'the hots' for her. She doesn't even realize how sexy she is either. She knocks me out."

"You sound love sick." Lee chuckled. "I have an idea our little sis feels the same way about you. What have you done to deserve such a break? And what are you doing about it?"

"I haven't done anything. What can I do? And what you call a break, feels more like heartbreak to me." Dell groaned as he applied pressure to the pliers, twisting the wire securely to hold the gaping break securely.

"You should romance the girl."

Dell shook his head. "I'm a struggling artist who didn't even finish college. I have nothing to offer her. No home, no money, no secure future. I'm younger than she is. What else could I have against me? The deck is stacked, man."

"Cindi doesn't care about money. Cindi respects talent. How is your work? Are you any good?"

"You can judge for yourself when we get back to the house. I've got a lot of my paintings at the pool house. I can't judge my own work. If I say 'hell yes, I'm good' I sound like an egomaniac. If I say 'I'm no damn good' I sound like a fool. I only know I have to paint or die. Cindi's father encourages me. He likes my stuff." Dell mentally made a note to cover his latest painting before he allowed Lee to view his work.

"You sound like some of my friends back home in Lake Charles. Have you tried to get a gallery to accept your work for a show? Do you have an agent?"

"Now you sound like Cindi. That's what she said after looking at my work. Miss Flowers was acting as my agent. She's been talking to a place in Shreveport. They have some of my stuff. Maybe I'll hear from them soon."

"Don't say you have nothing to offer, then," Lee chided. "If Cindi cares about you at all, you've got a real shot with her. Like I said before, money and material things aren't important to her. She lives for her music. And she could teach anywhere. She's not bound to that school in California by any means."

The two men continued on their patrol of the grounds. Dell mulled over Lee's words with a hopeful attitude. Maybe there might be a way to win Cindi for his own.

After a time of companionable silence, Dell decided to ask Lee what he knew of the way Cliff had treated Cindi. It was such a sensitive subject he wasn't sure how to broach it, but before he could say a word, Lee began to talk about it.

"Have you met Cliff Aymond?"

"Funny, you should ask that. I was just trying to get up the courage to ask you about him and Cindi. What happened to break them up?"

"I don't know the whole story," Lee answered. "All I really know is that Cindi confided in my mother and me that she and Cliff were going to elope. Cindi was only seventeen at the time. Just about to graduate from high school and planning to attend college on a full scholarship. Of course my mother advised her against it. Then the next thing we knew, Cindi had done it."

"Done it? You mean they actually married. I thought they were only engaged."

"Uh, they were. Maybe I should have said eloped. They ran off, but they didn't get married. In fact, I'm not sure Cliff even thought of them as engaged to be married. It was just a line to get to Cindi. He's such a snake."

"You mean he was stringing her along all the time?" A furious scowl covered Dell's darkened face. "If you ask me, he's worse than a snake. He must think he's God's gift to women because now he's doing the same thing to Rita."

"Are you talking about the gal who cooked our lunch? He is a creep. Too bad we can't somehow give him a taste of his own medicine."

"Maybe I can think of some way to fix him up," Dell muttered. *Like proving him guilty of murder and smuggling dope. That would put the skids to his race for the governorship of Louisiana.*

"Are we done now?" Lee asked.

"Sure, let's head back to the house."

Dell wanted to continue on to check out the Carver landing strip. He wanted to see if any large cartons or other evidence of the shipment could be seen. The only way he could do that was to be sneaky. He wasn't sure what Lee would think if he started skulking around. He'd just have to go back later alone.

* * *

When Lee and Dell left, Cindi and Marie retired to the master suite to talk. Years of gossip about mutual friends needed to be shared. Years of catching up on each other as well.

"This is a remarkable, gorgeous house." Miss Marie said when they were settled comfortably in the sitting room there. "Your father did a spectacular job when he designed it. The fact that it is haunted adds a piquant flavor to its beauty. I especially love the indoor garden. And this suite," Marie stopped and raised her hands and shoulders in a Gallic shrug. "Being able to lie in bed here in your room and look at the garden must be almost heaven."

Cindi smiled. She loved watching her teacher talk. "It's heaven," she responded. "Unless there's a big, black panther staring back through the glass. I haven't actually seen the animal, mind you. Local legend says it may appear, though. Then just as quickly vanish. The same thing happened to the pianist I told you of earlier. Somehow, for me the ghosts only have appeal during the daylight hours."

"Do you think these are really supernatural happenings? Or someone playing a trick."

Cindi shrugged. Somehow her shrug lacked the Frenchness of

Marie's. "I've tried to make them seem commonplace occurrences, but somehow there is a thread of uncanny, eerie feeling about the place. I can't explain it. It even extends to the graveyard of the nearby church."

"Do you think anything will happen this weekend?" Marie's voice held a note of hope.

Cindi smiled again. "You almost sound as if you hope something will happen. I'm not sure how I feel about that. Maybe these things are being staged. Cliff and Rita are probably the culprits if that's so."

"Why do you say that?"

"Dell overheard them talking. He thinks something might have happened to Consuelo Flowers, the owner of the house. And Cliff told me my father died in an escape attempt." She stopped, then added quickly, "But I don't believe him."

"Oh no. When did this happen?"

"Cliff just told me that yesterday."

"And you're not over the grief of your mother's passing yet. To lose your father would be too much. I'm not even going to allow myself to consider such a possibility. And what do you mean when you say something may have happened to Consuelo Flowers?"

"I believe Dell is afraid Cliff has murdered her or done something to her. He overheard Rita and Cliff talking about her. Cliff says she disappeared either on the trip to Colombia or after she arrived there."

"If that's true, when did it happen? Where is the body? Can you prove he did it?"

This time Cindi laughed full out. "We don't even know for sure that's she's dead. How can we go about learning the answers to all those questions of yours?"

"I'm a frustrated detective, my dear."

"I've got to ask you something. I've waited long enough. I want to know what you really think of Dell Comeaux. Your good opinion of him is very important to me. He really makes me hot and bothered."

"From what I've seen, he must be a remarkable young man. And I can tell he's as crazy about you as you are about him. Be honest now, girl. Aren't you in love with him?"

"Boy, do you have tough questions. Does it show that much? He's too young for me. He's only twenty. But there seems to be no age gap between us. What there is between us, is something magical. I'm sorry to say, though, that Dell acts, and talks, as though there is no future for us."

"He probably just wants to have prospects of being able to support himself, and you, in some substantial fashion before he allows himself to feel there can be a future for you two. As for the age difference, you're only twenty-three, my dear. That's not really an age gap. Age is not important." Marie stood and strolled around the room. "My own husband was two years younger than me," she continued in a musing tone as she paced. "I'm sure you never even realized that. We had twenty wonderful years together before he died. With me being older, I always expected to die first. I should have. I still miss him. If you truly love Dell, don't waste time, Cindi."

"I'll remember what you've said." Cindi thought things were getting too intense, so she changed the subject. She rose and moved over to the display of pianos and framed manuscripts. "I'd like to show you some of Consuelo's treasures. Here are original manuscripts of George Gershwin and Aaron Copeland. And do examine these precious jeweled pianos."

Cindi wanted to show off the beautiful musical memorabilia Consuelo owned. She also was anxious to stop discussing her feelings for Dell Comeaux. Funny, she had imagined she wanted to hear Miss Marie's opinion of Dell, but instead she'd discovered she just wanted to keep her own opinion safe from anyone else's.

Lost in her thoughts, Miss Marie startled her with her next remark.

"Your father drew these. Where did they come from?" She was holding the sketches Cindi had gotten from Rita.

"Uh, Rita gave them to me. To me, they're proof she worked for him in Colombia, and that he was alive when she left the country even though imprisoned. Rita claims he asked her to tell me to stay at Magnolia House, but I have no idea how he could have known I was here."

"You're wise to question that woman's motives. Look, Cindi. I think a word's been erased from the bottom of this sketch." She held out the sketch so Cindi could see. "Look, there was another word after this word. Prim, strange that's an English word since the others are all Spanish."

Miss Marie used her pince-nez to examine the picture more closely. "I think I can almost make it out. Yes, I can. It's era."

"Prim? Era? That doesn't make sense."

"Not prim era, it's one word—*primera*. That's Spanish for cousin. First cousin. Could your father have meant something by this?"

Cindi shrugged and looked thoughtful. "First cousin. Are Rita and Consuelo cousins? You know I've noticed a resemblance between Rita and Consuelo from that portrait in the living room. It's the smile. Sometimes Rita wears the same smile as Consuelo's painted one. To me, it's a smug, cruel smile. A smile that makes me wonder about Consuelo as well. Dell speaks fondly of her, but is—or was—she a person who could be trusted?" Cindi placed a hand to her throbbing throat. She had been talking too much.

"Your questioning spirit is the same as when you were a child, dear. I used to wonder if I would ever be able to answer all your questions about music and the piano. But I believe you are right about Rita and Consuelo. There is a resemblance. They could be cousins. As for Consuelo's real personality…" Miss Marie gave her shrug again. She flattened her mouth as if to add "Who knows?" Or perhaps the Frenchman's favorite standby, "*Pour quoi*?"

CHAPTER 11

Music from the piano spilled into Cindi's room and drew her attention with its purity and passion. She recognized the piece as one of Rachmaninoff's preludes. Prelude in C# to be exact. Such finger spans were beyond her own reach and so the musical piece was not in her repertoire. Music was on the menu for tonight, but not planned until after dessert and coffee. Someone had decided to skip the food courses.

She was expecting Samantha Carver and her husband, Jeff, at any moment. Whoever offered such glorious music before all had arrived was being hasty as well as impolite. And this was no mere practice warm-up, or casual, idle time-filler. This was a worthy performance.

Cindi wondered who was playing. She couldn't put a finger on who was making the glorious music. Definitely not Miss Marie. Her small hands couldn't manage those extended chords either. Not Lee either, unless his technique had greatly improved in the past two years. She started from her room with every intention of urging the performer to wait for a larger, more attentive audience.

She ran smack into Dell. He stood stock still as if the impact that brought their bodies together had rooted him to the spot. A strong flowery scent rose from something in his hands. Something he was lifting toward her hair.

Cindi followed the movement of his hands with her eyes. She glimpsed a cluster of pink rosebuds. Their slightly bruised and crushed petals gave off the rich aroma, which surrounded her and Dell.

"They suit you, *querida*," he muttered, using Spanish to guard his emotions from Cindi. He tucked the stems of the rosebuds into her upswept hair, brushing aside a curling, loose tendril, which coiled around his finger with a stubborn will of its own. "They're just your color."

Dell meant the shade of Cindi's nipples, whose erect peaks even now showed her response to his nearness. He could see them jutting through the soft knit of her oversized, light blue sweater. His intimate knowledge of their exact color was his own guilty secret, and he guarded that well. His fingers adjusted the position of the flowers as he struggled for control.

His gaze was drawn downwards as if to confirm his memory of the shade, but though the shape was evident, the sweater hid the color. The tempting upper curves of her breasts captured his attention then. He found he couldn't force himself to glance back up to her face, or leave his view of the tawny rich tan of her neck and shoulders revealed by the loose, low cowl neck of her sweater.

With a deep groan, he drew Cindi closer so that each part of their bodies nestled and fit firmly into each other. His lips found her shoulders and her throat, pressing kisses everywhere as he moved his mouth downward.

Cindi was almost melting from his touch. She twined her own arms around him and moved even closer. Her body felt boneless and subject to Dell's every whim. Then, out of nowhere, a glacial, vagrant breath of air touched the nape of her neck. Like an icy fingertip, the draft confused her, stiffened her spine. She realized with a sense of loss that the music had ceased. Perhaps it had only been a recording. She moaned softly, and whispered Dell's name.

"What is it, my sweet?" Dell whispered in return.

"Something is wrong. Something's here. Something out of place."

"Ssh, darling. *Usted es mi amante."* Dell told her. He wanted to reveal his love for her, but was afraid to speak it plainly.

"Where did those words come from?" Cindi objected. "You know Spanish is not my native tongue. I'm barely vocal in the language so I'm not sure what you've just said." But she knew the words sounded slightly indecent and definitely loving. Just the sound of them sent chills down her spine.

Another icy breeze swept over her, causing a different sort of chill. "There's that draft again," she squealed.

Dell's first impulse was to draw her yet closer if possible, and somehow comfort her fears away. Instead he moved away from her, held her at arms' length, and searched her face. With dawning comprehension penetrating through the haze of his own passionate feelings, he saw fear now gripped her instead. It showed in her eyes.

Dell felt a wisp of the frigid draft touch his own back. "You're right. Something isn't right. Must be something wrong with the air conditioning. I'll have to check on it."

Before he could carry out his plan, he saw Cindi's eyes widen and focus into a startled stare directed at the glass atrium wall behind him.

Then, the peal of the front door bell sounded.

Keeping his hands reassuringly on Cindi's arms, Dell turned his head in the direction of her gaze. He saw no sign of any unearthly specter there. Nothing to produce such fright.

"Nothing's there. Not a thing but a garden full of plants. What did you see? What startled you?"

"I'm not sure, but I am sure that's Samantha and her husband at the door," she gasped faintly as the bell pealed again. "We'll have to let them in, Dell. I think I saw—I, uh, I'm afraid the panther's back again."

"We're having a party and that damned beast is on the prowl? I don't want to believe this."

"Is it gone yet? Please tell me it's gone." Cindi fastened her eyes on Dell's face, searching for reactions that might signify he'd seen the beast.

At his absence of fright and affirmative nod to her plea, she gathered strength and courage. "I'm going to let them in then," she declared.

The doorbell pealed one more time. "It'll be all right," she said trying to reassure herself. But her panicky mind went on reasoning. *Yes, we can stay out on the deck for most of the party. I've never felt the least hint of anything spooky out there. Just stay cool.* To Dell she said, "How do I look?"

"You look gorgeous, babe. Go get 'em." Dell's sexy smile encouraged her as he lightly touched her cheek. "I'll go check the air conditioner in case there's something wrong with it. That will give me a few more minutes grace before I have to face the Carvers."

* * *

Greeting Jeff and Samantha Carver, she had given them a smile as stiff as plastic. They seemed to notice nothing. As Cindi shook Jeff's hand, she studied the man who looked nothing like the picture she'd made of him in her mind. This man looked nothing like the adventurer type you'd expect to be running a helicopter service. Instead of relaxed, casual clothes, he wore a pinstriped, long sleeve shirt. His chino Dockers were crisply pressed, belying the garment's reputation of comfort. The man's carefully combed, sandy hair held a rigid part. His mouth and expression were obscured by a bushy, full mustache, and he exuded vigilance and readiness.

He looks prepared for anything, including an attack by the Loggy Branch monster. She choked back an inappropriate giggle. Classifying the man as a pompous ass, a "stuffed shirt", she drew Jeff and Samantha into the house. As if on cue, Marie and Lee appeared on the stairs just then. The party had begun.

They'd made their way to the rear deck as Cindi had planned. The quiet and beauty there were undisturbed. At last she let her earlier fears for the evening subside.

Sitting there, she looked out at the soft lights shining in and around the pool, making it glow like an iridescent jewel. Citronella candles burned on the deck, discouraging mosquitoes. In the romantic dimness, Cindi breathed a sigh of relief and relaxed. Her nerves had been in a jangle since the moment she bumped into Dell. Jangled because of desire for Dell, jangled because of fear of the phantom beast that walked the atrium.

Dell, who sat next to her, took her relaxation as a sign. In an intimate way, he leaned over and pulled her arm through his. Comforted and warmed by his action, she smiled. She wished she and Dell were alone together somewhere.

For now, it was enough that her party was going well. She steeled herself to perform her duty to her guests. Her glance moved from person to person starting with a special sidelong, downcast look and a demure, promising smile for Dell.

Samantha and Jeff Carver sat next to Dell. Side by side on a cushioned bench, they faced away from the pool. Jeff sat rigidly upright, his pants still perfectly creased, his hair unruffled by the light breeze. Cindi decided he must have used hair spray on it. Not a whisker of his bristling mustache was ruffled either. He showed no noticeable emotion except when his gaze chanced to light on Dell. Then he bristled all over with ill will. Cindi wished she'd realized there might be bad blood between the two men. She was glad she and Samantha were buffers between them.

Samantha leaned comfortably against the rail. The woman's face bore a calmer mien, her eyes a less somber expression tonight.

Lee sat next to Jeff, then Miss Marie sat just beyond, creating a loose semi-circle. Conversation flowed easily among everyone and in soft asides between those seated next to each other. Yes, all was going well. She relaxed even more.

As Cindi's gaze circled the group again, her confidence fled. Her hands gripped the arms of her chair, she drew in an involuntary breath. She spied an alien, additional figure. To Marie's left, and set back from the group, an insubstantial shape reclined in a chaise lounge in the gloom. It was a young woman. As Cindi strained to make out her features which seemed to shift and move, she realized the woman was no one she had ever seen before. No one she knew.

The young lady, hardly more than a girl, looked straight at Cindi. Her features grew more solid. Her eyes glowed and held Cindi's gaze for a long moment. As soft as a sigh, the name Cordelia slipped into her mind. No one else gave evidence of having seen the additional guest. All hell would break loose if they did, for Cindi felt her certainty of the apparition's identity grow. As their gazes remained locked, she saw a subtle look of satisfaction cross the girl's face. Cordelia nodded slightly as if to affirm Cindi's knowledge of her identity.

Her attention wavered from the specter as Dell's sweet breath rippled through her hair and across her ear. It brought warmth to her cheeks and deep in the pit of her stomach tremors rippled and knotted. Her reaction to him distracted her from the ghostly figure.

"I hear Tai cutting up over at my house. I'm going to slip over to quiet him. I'll get my guitar while I'm there. Come with me, babe."

"I can't. A good hostess never leaves her guests. Go on. When you get back, we'll start the music." Cindi prayed Dell would not see Cordelia. She couldn't bear to see that soft expression of love she'd grown used to fill his eyes at the sight of another woman.

Dell pulled her hand to his lips. He pressed a kiss there before releasing her arm and rising to leave. He showed no sign of noticing anyone but her.

"Miss Marie, would you play first?" Cindi asked her teacher. "Dell is getting his guitar. I suggest we go on in and gather around the piano. We'll have an old-fashioned sing-along. Just don't expect to hear my voice above a very discreet hum."

Lee left the group as well to return quickly with a small electric keyboard, which he set up on the closed top of the Steinway. Dell returned and the music began.

Miss Marie played solo for some fifteen minutes. She beckoned to

Lee to join her as she turned from the classics to Broadway show tunes. Soon Dell joined in, and everyone, except for Cindi, sang along.

"Cindi, your turn," Miss Marie said.

Cindi took her place at the piano. She started with a collection of her own original tunes. Dell followed her lead with harmonizing chords. She swung into boogie-woogie and rock and roll classics. Dell's guitar came alive as he improvised hot licks and riffs while jamming with her. Lee set up a punishing bass on the keyboard. The formal setting came unglued; the joint began to jump.

When Cindi began to play old and new pop favorites, even Rita joined in with her off-key singing. Making coffee in the silver pot, Rita sang along with everything she recognized. After arranging an assorted array of goodies and sweets, she stayed on. Though she exited briefly to bring in a carafe of *café con leche*, she joined the group when she returned. In a quieter mode than usual, Rita continued to add her voice to the others. Cindi was overjoyed to see Rita recovering her usual verve and boisterous spirits.

Lee and Dell took their turn next. They played old country standards and folk songs.

"How about you two?" Cindi asked Samantha and Jeff.

"Oh, no, sorry," Samantha answered and laughed. "We love music, but you would hate any sounds we made."

The music seemed to be done when Cindi felt inspiration strike. "Rita, would you like to sing or play something?"

Rita nodded and went to the piano. She seated herself and adjusted the bench. She appeared on edge and nervous. Her first chords brought complete silence. They were the magnificent opening ones of the Rachmaninoff prelude Cindi had heard earlier. Rita's rendition was masterful and kept the audience spellbound. Afterward, she tacked on a medley of Spanish folk songs that set her listeners singing again and clapping along.

"You've certainly been hiding your talent," Cindi commented to Rita as they moved to the spread of desserts. "That was a superb ending to our musical evening." She turned to the others. "Come on, folks, it's time for coffee and dessert."

When she turned back, Rita was gone. Cindi planned to pin Rita down and ask about her earlier session at the keyboard when the guests cleared out.

In the general flurry of serving the desserts and coffee, Cindi didn't wonder where Rita had gone. At first Cindi just felt annoyed at Rita's absence. The full burden of making sure everyone got something to eat and drink now fell on her. She decided Rita must be suffering from delayed shyness over her stunning conclusion to the recital. So, at first, she didn't worry. After all, Rita had stolen the show. Ability such as she had displayed went beyond inborn talent, and usually came only with years of practice and lessons. Such training belied Rita's claim to be merely a poor servant, making Cindi wonder how much of anything Rita had told her was true.

After the Carvers left and Lee and Marie went up to bed, Cindi and Dell cleaned up the mess from the party.

Rita still hadn't shown.

"She pouted and sulked all day. Now she's neglecting her duties just when she could really be of use," Cindi fumed to Dell.

"You could always go up to her room and drag her back down here. Of course Ravin' Rita would probably make a bunch of noise about that."

"I'm sure she would. It would just disturb Miss Marie and Lee, too. I'm sure they are both tired. And to tell the truth, it's nice to be alone with you."

Dell winked one eye and grabbed her. "It's very nice working with you." He pinned her against the counter and pulled her tightly into his arms. "You don't know what you do to me. You don't have any idea how desirable you are. All night I've been wanting to get you alone."

"We're alone now. Show me what I do to you." In addition to her spoken invitation, she twined her arms around his neck. "Kiss me, Dell."

Dell bent his lips to her parted ones and lazily brushed them. An electric tingle snaked down Cindi's spine. Dell lifted his hand to the rosebuds nestled in her hair. He cupped the back of her head and crushed their lips together. His other hand drifted to her breast where he stroked and teased her erect nipple with his thumb. Flames radiated from there to every part of her body, finally gravitating to her very center.

Cindi welcomed his kisses, his caresses. She hardly dared breathe, she hardly was able to breathe. Finally she pulled back, trying to put space between them. His touch was drugging her, causing her to forget the things that still were undone.

"Darling, please. Let's please finish loading the dishwasher."

Dell sighed. "You're right. We've still got work ahead of us. You go check the living room and see if we've brought all the dishes from there. I'll get the rest of them in the dishwasher and straighten the kitchen."

Wearing a radiant glow, Cindi moved about the formal areas. Setting the house back to rights, with only Dell's company and help, gave her a glimpse of what living with Dell might be like. Alone with him as they performed domestic chores, the atmosphere proved both intimate and curiously domestic, as though they were an ordinary, long-married couple.

"I'll see you in the morning, babe," Dell said when they finished. "I'll be over likely before you're even up to see about breakfast. Maybe Ravin' Rita will be up and ready to help, maybe not."

"Goodnight, Dell." Cindi let her lips brush his in the lightest way, and lifted her hand to caress his cheek. He caught her hand and pressed a kiss in her palm.

"Goodnight, *querida. Usted es mi amante."*

In a dreamy haze, Cindi remained transfixed by the French door where Dell had left her. That certainly sounded like a Spanish "I love you", she thought. She made a note to find a Spanish dictionary. Then she drifted to her room where sleep embraced her. Sleep and dreams of Dell Comeaux.

CHAPTER 12

After only a couple of hours sleep, Cindi woke up. No unearthly music or ghostly voices, only the rising wind outside, and perhaps the faintest far-off creaking disturbed the quietness of her room. She moved uneasily in her bed. Once again something seemed wrong, alien. Had Cordelia returned? She told herself it was probably Rita who'd returned instead, perhaps from a rendezvous with Cliff. But whatever was the cause, she didn't think she would be able to go back to sleep. She wished Dell were there to hold her and make her feel safe.

To get her thoughts off Dell, Cindi went back over the party in her mind. Cordelia's face surfaced. All the excitement of the music and Rita's outstanding performance had driven that ghostly sighting from her remembrance for hours. Until now. Wrapping a light robe around herself, she rose and moved uneasily through the darkened suite.

Her wanderings led her through the private sitting room and solarium. There she halted and hesitated before the French doors that led out onto the suite's patio. She was lured by the peaceful beauty of the outside. The bright moonlight bathed the scene before her in a calm, serene light even as the light breeze that moved through the trees promised respite from her heated recollections.

Still inside, she glanced back uneasily at the shadowy rooms behind her. She hadn't turned on any lights. The moonlight shining through the skylights had been enough to guide her through the familiar rooms. Now, fantastic dark shapes moved on the walls of the small sitting room and bedroom beyond. She knew they were thrown there by the moon and moved by the capricious wind that rustled through the stiff, oval leaves of the banana trees growing in the corners of the patio. Still, sudden, irrational fear leaped in her throat at the sight. The outside suddenly seemed safer than the confines of Magnolia House.

Fear and excitement mingled in her mind as she thought of Dell's kisses and teasing love play. Her remembrances brought every sense in her body to fever pitch. Longing for Dell fizzed and crackled through her blood bringing heat to her body and face as she relived his touches and his kisses.

With her head turned toward those frightening shadows in the room, Cindi stepped through the door directly into Dell's waiting arms. Her startled gasp and subsequent relieved sigh as she recognized his unique scent, left her trembling and weak with heightened desire.

"I guess I should be getting used to walking through doors and bumping into you. What were you doing? Hiding among the banana trees to spy on me?"

Dell's eyes showed hurt. "I was checking the locks on all the doors and looking over the grounds before I went to bed. I had just walked up to check your doors. What are you doing up?"

"I woke up and couldn't get back to sleep. I wasn't scared until you grabbed me." Cindi knew she was lying, but how could she tell Dell she had seen Cordelia?

"Come on," Dell urged. "I'm sorry I scared you. Let's sit a while and talk. Since you can't sleep, we might as well use the time for talking. I've got something to tell you."

He led her to a bench near the gate and steps that led up to the rear deck. Somehow he seemed more solemn and subdued than earlier in the kitchen as they worked together. He made no attempt to kiss her or caress her, or even put his arm around her shoulders. He simply sat apart from her, facing her and holding her hands loosely. His gaze lingered on her face. The bright moonlight lent his own face a beauty that seemed other worldly.

"What do you want to tell me?" Cindi asked. A foreboding sense of sadness crept over her. Her brain sifted through the things she imagined he might say. Her body grew cold all over. Even the warm, fragrant breeze failed to warm her.

He's going to tell me he only wants us to be friends. Or say I'm too old for him. Maybe he will tell me we shouldn't feel as we do about each other, like he did that day in the garage. He's going to break my heart.

But she was wrong.

Dell paused, collecting his thoughts. He studied Cindi's face as if he must memorize it. He began speaking slowly, choosing his words with care. "I'd just like to tell you what really happened the night Cordelia Carver died. I guess I'm going to have to start by telling you about her family. Seeing her parents here tonight brought it all back to me. Her father really hates me, so I try to stay out of his way as much as I can. I haven't seen him since the funeral."

He kept his loose grip on Cindi's hands, while his gaze held her attention. She fought for breath as she waited to hear words that might splinter and shatter her heart. This was going to be much worse than she had imagined.

Don't let him tell me he'll never be able to love anyone like he did Cordelia. I can't lose Dell, too.

Scratching, and whining cries from the other side of the gate broke their rapt focus on each other. The gate wasn't latched. Cindi saw it move, and Tai's distinctive shape squirmed through. He came straight to her and laid his great head in her lap. Absently she fondled his ears and rubbed the folds of skin on his neck. He lay uneasily at her feet as she reached down to continue petting him.

"I'd really like to hear about Cordelia," Cindi prompted. "Her parents, too. They both seem so troubled."

"Okay. To start with, now you know they live on the west boundary of Miss Flowers' land. I've never taken you that direction on a hike because Jeff Carver has forbidden me to enter his property. I don't strictly stay off, but I would never bring you with me when I go there at times to paint. I don't want you to face an unpleasant scene if he found us on his place."

"Afraid I couldn't handle it, huh?"

Dell smiled. "I'm sure you could, I just don't want you to have to. The run-down farmhouse where they live has been in the Carver family for generations. Cordelia was their only child. That's one reason he hates me so."

Cindi nodded. "I understand. He blames you for her death."

Dell nodded in return and continued. "Samantha has always worked to help out with money because Jeff has never been able to really make a go at farming. When the library opened in Ida, she moved from the main library in Shreveport to this one here. Things got a little better for Cordelia then. At least her mother was home more.

"Financially things got a little better for them then, too. Jeff decided to try something new. He'd been a helicopter pilot in Desert Storm. He put in a landing strip, and opened a helicopter service on his back forty. I wondered where he got the money to start up his business, and Cordelia told me Miss Flowers was a silent partner in the business.

"Anyway, to make a long story short, Cordelia and I got to be friends because neither of our families were really there for us.

"Mine were always off on missionary trips saving the 'heathen,' and you've seen for yourself how self-absorbed hers are."

Cindi had to show her agreement. "I know what it's like to have a family like that. I grew up in one myself. I always felt I was my mother's parent instead of her child. Then my dad left us, so I had to take care of her all on my own," she burst in. She put her arms around Dell. Knowing that she found comfort and warmth, a sense of peace and safety in his arms, she longed to give him the same by holding him.

Dell gave her a sweet smile, and hugged her back. He kept his own arms around her. He went on with his story.

"When we started high school, we both had to ride the school bus twenty miles or so to a big consolidated school in another town. Ida School only goes to the eighth grade. It was just natural that we got thrown together, but Cordelia was never more than a friend to me. I called her my girl friend when I told you and Rita about the wreck, but she wasn't really. There was nothing romantic between us."

"So you didn't love her?"

Dell shook his head. "She was just my friend."

The relieved sigh that Cindi gave startled Dell, but he went on with his story.

"I found out Jeff Carver's helicopter service was a cover-up for smuggling. Miss Flowers had people in Colombia who needed to get certain persons and certain things to the United States. She used Jeff's service for that. But Cordelia's father added cocaine to their cargo list. I'm not sure if Miss Flowers knew this when he started it. From things she said, I believe she only found out about the drugs a short time before she left for Colombia."

Cindi prompted him once again. "So the smuggling started as a means of getting emeralds into the country illegally? And coffee? People? What kind of people?"

"Illegal aliens, desperate people in search of better jobs and freedom."

"And Jeff added cocaine. Could Rita and Cliff be in this scheme with him? Could this be behind Consuelo's disappearance?"

"I'm pretty sure Rita and Cliff are in with Jeff since I heard him talking about that shipment. And to your second question, I guess so. And maybe we'll never see Rita again either. Her job here might be finished."

"I agree. I think."

"You've got to let me finish. I haven't even told you about the night Cordelia was killed."

Cindi nodded and snuggled her head into the muscular curve of Dell's shoulder. "I'm listening," she said.

"Jeff got Cordelia hooked on drugs. He was supplying her. I never realized it till after she died. I don't think the crash killed her. She must have used cocaine or something that night before I picked her up." Dell stopped for a moment. He took a deep breath. "I put some wine coolers and beer on ice in my car that night instead of the soda pop I usually filled my ice chest with. My plan was to get her high on the booze and see how far I could go with her."

Cindi shifted in his arms. She stared at him, but didn't speak.

"Don't look at me that way. Please. Listen to the rest of it. Remember I was a lot younger. It was a dumb teenage stunt."

Cindi spoke hurried words of comfort. "I remember my own teenage fling with Cliff. My own thinking was muddled when I was that age. Tell me the rest of it." She settled back into her earlier position in his arms.

Dell absently stroked Cindi's hair and continued. "I couldn't go through with my plan. Cordelia was just a good friend. I knew it was wrong to even think of using her friendship that way." Dell's focus turned inward, and he withdrew into himself, but went on. "As I've already said, when I picked her up that night she was already spaced out. We rode around a while. She said she was thirsty and reached around to get something to drink from the ice chest. Before I knew it, she was drinking wine coolers like they were water. She passed out and her breathing got slower and slower. I got scared. I didn't know what else to do, so I was on the way to take her home and you know the rest."

"You saw the panther and lost control of the car?"

"Right, but like I said I found out that the crash didn't kill her because she was already dead from the combination of drugs and alcohol. She overdosed. So in appearance it was as much my fault as it was the animal's sudden appearance in the road. Jeff just greased the right palms and fixed the coroner's report so that the crash was listed as the cause of death. He did it to hide his own dirty secret."

"How? How can you be so sure?"

"I made it my business to find out," Dell said, speaking once again in a flat monotone. "It was quite a while before I began to suspect anything. The first week or so I was numb and torn up."

"Then what?"

"She had a gash on her head from the impact. At first I didn't question the coroner's verdict. I was just glad I hadn't been jailed for supplying alcohol to a minor. Thank the Lord, I hadn't been drinking any of it myself, or that would have been against me. Later on I realized there hadn't been much blood from her wound. It hadn't gushed or poured out.

"My parents, especially my mom, were insistent that I get a job and help pay the automobile insurance which went sky-high after my wreck. So I got a part-time job after school at the sheriff's sub station. Eventually I got curious and took a look at the coroner's report. It was easy to see it had been changed."

Cindi's mind slowly absorbed and processed all the things Dell had told her. She allowed a rising hope to warm her heart. She began to smile.

"What's this? You're smiling. How can you smile when I've just told you about the most awful night I ever lived through?" Dell's voice signified disgust. For once Cindi's true feelings were hidden from him.

"Oh, Dell, I know it was awful for you. I'm sorry. I can see you've been tormented by these memories. I know you blame yourself. You really shouldn't, though."

"Then what? Why the Mona Lisa smile?"

"The smile is because I thought you really loved Cordelia so much you would never be able to love or want me the way I love and want you."

"Don't you know how I feel about you?" Dell crushed her roughly in his arms in his haste to reassure her. Doubts and fears of his involvement with her fled as he kissed her with all the hunger he'd been feeling for her. He still couldn't put his feelings into words though.

Cindi steeled her rapidly dissolving will. She would not be fooled by another man. She twisted out of his arms demanding, "I'd like to hear how you feel about me."

"Cindi, don't. It's too soon. If you can't feel the truth and strength of my affection for you, I'll have to leave."

"If you can't speak plainly to me of love, go."

Dell sighed, dropped his arms which he'd been holding out to her. "Come on, Tai. Let's go home."

Cindi rushed back into the house sobbing. Why did love have to hurt so? She wished she could die from the pain of her broken heart. Would no man ever love her enough?

She cried herself to sleep.

Dell worked as if possessed through the night. He went as far as he could with the last painting he'd started of Cindi.

Sometimes he wept, too.

CHAPTER 13

Cindi woke from her restless, broken sleep. Last night, each time she and Dell had been alone together, his kisses and embraces raised her hopes. Then his lack of words dashed them. She knew she loved him. She wanted to believe he loved her, but hardly dared believe. Could she believe him? Could she trust him when he didn't say the words of love she needed to hear?

Noises came from the kitchen. Not loud banging or singing that would point to Rita, but small stirring noises. The creak of a pantry door, the sound of a pot on the stove. A wonderful smell of crisping bacon wafted through the air.

Dell must be the breakfast chef this morning, she decided. They had worked so well together last night, maybe he needed her help. Thoughts of their recent camaraderie brought back memories of their kisses. Cindi lit up when she remembered them. The expectance of Dell's good morning hug and kiss surely waiting her in the kitchen sent hope surging through her heart. All her tears and disappointment were forgotten. She hurried through her shower and dressed.

"Good morning, Cindi," Miss Marie called from the hall outside Cindi's room just as Cindi was ready to head for the kitchen.

"Good morning. I hope you had a good night's rest, Miss Marie." Despite her courteous greeting, Cindi felt disappointed that she would have no time alone with Dell. She wondered why she had ever imagined having guests would be nice.

"Is that Riotous Rita in the kitchen?" her teacher asked.

Cindi laughed. "It's Dell. Rita makes more noise. That's why Dell calls her Ravin' Rita. I don't think anyone has seen her since shortly after her performance last night."

"She performed very well. Have you checked to see if she is still asleep?"

"I'm afraid I haven't. Last night I was afraid to. She might have raised a fuss. As hired help goes, she is very independent. Seems to think she was born to a better station in life."

"I'll go up and knock on her door," Miss Marie offered. "You go and see if the coffee is ready."

"I'll do that." Cindi blessed Miss Marie for giving her a chance to be with Dell alone even if only for a moment. She made the most of her time by creeping in to surprise him with kisses on the back of his neck.

Dell dropped his spatula and turned to grab her and give her a proper good morning kiss.

As soon as she could, Cindi moved out of his grasp. "Miss Marie is up. She'll be down in just a few minutes. She's checking on Rita, but she's ready for her first cup of coffee so she won't be long."

"The coffee's ready, but I don't think she'll find a trace of Rita. I think that lady has vacated the premises."

"No, I didn't find her," Miss Marie said as she entered the kitchen. "I opened the door a crack. Her bed hasn't been disturbed and the room has an empty feel. I think the riotous one has gone."

"She must be with Cliff after all." Cindi filled Miss Marie in on Cliff and Rita.

After breakfast, Lee and Dell left to walk the property lines. Miss Marie and Cindi took an early morning dip in the pool. Afterward, they sat on the master suite patio in the sun to dry off.

"Cindi, you've got to accept your feelings for Dell. Don't let past failed relationships spoil your chances with him."

"But what should I do? Soon I'll have to go back to the West Coast. My sick leave won't last forever. I don't want to leave Dell, but he hasn't said he wants me to stay."

"Trust your heart."

The two women relaxed and talked first in the sun and then in the shade of the secluded walled patio. Cindi let her hopes fill her heart. Maybe she could do what her teacher suggested.

Their time together passed quickly, and the Guidrozes were soon ready to leave for home.

"Goodbye, don't forget to write." they told her.

"Goodbye Miss Marie. Goodbye Lee. I'll plan to come to Lake Charles for a visit soon," Cindi promised.

"I'll be coming, too. See you soon," Dell added.

Cindi raised her eyebrows at his words, but kept her own counsel. The thought came to her that now her friends were leaving and Rita wasn't around, she and Dell would be alone together at Magnolia House.

* * *

"Tilt your head to the left just a bit more. Now lean back and try to look relaxed. One arm over your head...yes, that's okay."

Cindi managed to reach the exact position Dell had described. Dell whistled and said, "Wow, that's perfect."

His face full of fierce concentration, he turned back to his canvas and began to paint with quick, energetic strokes. Cindi likened his fast, impatient movements to a whirlwind ever in motion as he looked first at her then immediately back at the canvas. His movements reminded her of the ones he made in his morning exercises, rapid, yet controlled.

She dared take a deep breath. After the struggle to understand and follow Dell's detailed instructions on how she must pose, she needed a sustaining breath. She'd been holding back, fearing even the slightest movement of her chest would distract Dell. But now she knew she could be a bowl of fruit or a tree and he would never notice subtle movement. His attention was centered on his art. Oblivious to everything except the vision he wished to capture, he worked intently.

Keeping her body motionless while biting her tongue to keep from speaking, Cindi let her mind wander. Throughout the Guidrozes' visit, Magnolia House had been quiet. No haunts had publicly appeared to satisfy her guests' curiosity. The house had remained quiet.

Only she had seen the strange, ghostly girl on the deck the night of the recital. Only she had seen the panther in the atrium just before the Carvers arrived that same night. She decided both unsettling occurrences had been warning gestures meant for her eyes alone. She hadn't shared the sighting of the mysterious young woman with anyone. She would never tell Dell she believed Cordelia had come to join them that night. Only Dell knew she had seen the panther.

The night they talked on her patio, she almost confided in him about seeing Cordelia. Stopping at the last moment, she did so because she was almost certain he had told her the truth about his feelings for Cordelia. Almost. The trouble was, maybe his feelings for her weren't any stronger than the ones he'd had for the dead girl. After all, Cordelia continued to haunt Magnolia House. Perhaps she was bound here by Dell's strong feelings for her. The apparition had never seemed threatening. Rather Cordelia seemed to be satisfied just to know Cindi acknowledged her presence.

How could Cindi be sure of his feelings? In her heart, she knew she loved Dell. Perhaps he would never love her back. Perhaps he couldn't love her or any other woman. Though he embraced her and kissed her till she was limp with desire, the only words of love he had ever given her were spoken in a foreign tongue. Their meaning was unclear to her. Her scarred heart needed to know plainly that she was loved.

Trust your heart, Miss Marie had told her. But how could she?

Cindi resolutely refused to continue to obsess over the puzzling riddle. Turning her mind to another mysterious puzzle, she tried to figure out where Rita had gone. When the woman got up from the piano bench after her performance, she'd lingered only long enough to hear Cindi's comments and a general round of applause and compliments from the others. Then she left the room. She hadn't been seen since.

That night, no one even really saw her leave the room. There were no sounds of departure. Not even her heels clicking upon the stairs, the sharp sound of her bedroom door closing or the noise of a car engine had been heard. No sound drew their attention to her disappearance, but later she wasn't to be seen or found. She'd vanished quietly and completely.

Cindi's face flushed and her eyes glazed over as she remembered the intimacy she'd felt between herself and Dell as they cleaned up. Working alone together had been a sharing time. A mundane, homey experience that spoke to Cindi of closeness and bonding. She remembered Dell's kisses and caresses that complicated their simple tasks.

Cindi's dreamy, romantic expression got Dell's attention. He worked to capture it. He felt he knew the source of her rosy cheeks and the dazed expression in her eyes.

Only the presence of others in the house had stopped him the night of the musicale. Later that night on the patio, it had been even harder to resist her charms. Soon the effort to keep his passion and true feelings from Cindi would be impossible. But he must be able to promise her more than just his love then.

Remembering her warm lips and the passionate kisses they'd shared, awakened and stirred his desire for her. He couldn't keep his mind on his painting. His body throbbed. He longed, no more, he needed to throw down his brush and palette and take Cindi in his arms. Only her look of complete trust stopped him. Dell thought of Cliff and how he was with women. He frowned. She must be wooed with care. He must help her know she was worthy of an honorable man's love. He poured his tumultuous feelings into the work before him. Inspiration overtook him again and he translated his desire into every stroke he put on the canvas.

Cindi's tremulous sigh brought him back to reality.

"Babe, forgive me," he said. "I'm no better than a heartless pig. I forgot you and let you hold your pose too long. Relax for a moment, please."

Cindi relaxed. "I guess a selfish, heartless pig is better than a male chauvinist pig. I'm just a little stiff is all." She gave a languid stretch and started over to see the results of their session.

"Oh no, you don't," Dell said, stopping her short. "I don't want you to see it till I'm through. I'm superstitious about my work. Not when it's copied like the one I did from your little girl photograph, but when I paint from life."

Cindi pouted and made a face.

"You can see the little girl one. I'm through with it." Dell feared Cindi's reaction to the liberty he had taken of painting her nude. He led her over to the other painting.

"Here," he said, as he found the right stack and raised her completed youthful portrait high.

"Yep, that's me. Back when I was a little twerp," Cindi said and gave a long, lingering yawn and another stretch.

Dell's body quickened and heated at her movements. "Don't call yourself a twerp, Babe," he said.

"Oh yeah, who's going to stop me?"

Their playful exchange of words evaporated as Dell pulled Cindi into his arms. Covering her mouth with his own to stop her joking words, he found he couldn't stop there. He drew her even closer and rained kisses on her soft throat and shoulders. Cindi struggled half-heartedly to break his embrace, but tripped over Tai who lay sleeping on the floor. Tai yelped and raced for the open door.

Once she and Dell hit the floor, he rolled her beneath him and pinned her to the sisal mat covering. The heat Dell had felt as he painted the intimate details of Cindi's anatomy returned tenfold. He saw it matched in Cindi's flushed cheeks, and her softening, languorous touch.

Cindi longed to allow Dell full freedom of her body. She longed to allow him to enter and fill her. She had never felt this overwhelming need to be close, without boundaries, before. She knew she must hold him in that most intimate of all embraces, tight within her. Her eyes showed him her need. She heard his quick gasp as he understood it.

She closed her betraying eyes, but was unable to keep her lips from whispering his name with urgent appeal. "Dell, Dell," she murmured.

In her whisper, Dell heard the mockingbird's song to its mate. He heard the wind's loving caress of the magnolia tree. He heard a baby's cooing cry to its mother. But mostly he heard Cindi's deep longing to be loved and to give her love in return. He responded, beginning his sweet, hot kisses again.

Cindi moved against Dell's body. Her center melted, becoming molten hot and moist.

"Cindi, *querida*, let me love you. Let me make you mine." He corrected himself. "No, you are already mine. Let me claim what is mine."

"Yes, take me. I am yours," Cindi urged wordlessly. If he would not speak his love for her, at least she would know his loving.

Their kisses grew longer and deeper. Dell's tongue plundered Cindi's mouth. Her desire for their union grew. Her own tongue found and dueled with his. The unbearable fire in her belly grew apace.

Dell pulled back and looked into her eyes. He began to unbutton her shirt. Slowly he pushed the concealing garment away. Her lacy wisp of a bra barely contained her swollen breasts. He slid the straps off her shoulders.

Cindi dropped her gaze. "I never wanted you to see me like this." Even in her passion, the bright, sunlit room offended her innate modesty. In the harsh and revealing light, she shrank from his look falling on her lush curves.

"Why not, babe?" He pushed back her hair and rained kisses on her shoulders. "You look wonderful to me."

"Hideous and fat, you mean," she said and tried in vain to find her discarded clothes.

"Perfectly desirable and womanly, I say." He held her wrists together easily with one of his hands and kept her from accomplishing what she sought to do. He pulled her from the floor with his other hand and drew her into his tiny bathroom to view her nakedness. "I won't have you say anything bad about your beautiful body."

The love in his face was evident as his mirrored image reflected back at Cindi along with her own uncovered breasts, and disheveled clothing and hair. The reckless, wild look on her own face amazed her, taking her breath away.

"I like your opinion best. Have it your way." Cindi turned away from the revealing mirror to lose herself in Dell's arms. She threw caution to the winds. She was her father's daughter as she'd always feared. She might as well enjoy her wanton streak. She gave herself wholeheartedly to him. Her tremendous need to open to him, enfold him and draw him closer and tighter inside returned.

Dell moved away, and while continuing to stoke her breasts with one hand, took a small silver packet from a nearby dresser drawer. "I need to take care of you," he murmured. "Do you want me?"

"Yes, yes, you know I do," Cindi answered as she drew him back to her with one arm, all the while wriggling out of her jeans with the other.

The lovers, free of their constraining garments at last, embraced, feeling flesh against flesh. Cindi felt she might swoon with ecstasy as Dell's strong muscular body fit against her own softer curves. Together they dropped onto Dell's futon. As he began to enter her, she could hardly bear to wait to feel him inside her. Slowly, he began thrusting deeper and deeper. Cindi found his rhythm and matched it with the movement of her hips.

He dropped his mouth to suckle one upright nipple while his fingers caressed and teased the nipple of her other breast. He gave equal attention to each one. She laced her fingers through his hair and drew him tighter to her. Her legs clasped his waist. Together the two surged closer and closer to release. When it came, it tore through them both with ripple after ripple of blinding sensation. Cindi cried out Dell's name. He answered with hers.

Afterward they lay together quietly, locked in each other's arms as their hearts slowly resumed a more normal beat and their breathing eased.

Finally Cindi whispered Dell's name once more. She longed to hear words of love, but Dell refused to accommodate that need. Instead he stroked her hair in that tender way he had. Cindi took that comfort and was content.

* * *

"Dinner on the grounds," Cindi said as she and Dell bounced along in his truck on the way to St. Elisabeth Baptist Church. "I'm finally going to find out what that outrageous phrase means."

"It means just what it says," Dell said. "And the full title is 'all day singing and dinner on the grounds day.'"

Cindi gave a soft chuckle. "If everyone brings as much food as we have, it'll take all day to eat all of it." She gave a backward glance at the huge picnic basket crammed with fried chicken, corn casserole, white chocolate brownies, and whatever else edible Dell had found to add.

Tai sat near the basket, protecting it. Cindi met the dog's grinning gaze. Through the glass, she heard him whine. He jumped up and planted his short front legs on the lip of the truck bed. Pressing his nose against the back glass of the cab, his smiling, wide jaws took up so much room Cindi could no longer see the picnic basket.

"Sorry Tai, you've got to stay back there. But we'll soon be where we're going."

So soon, I'm getting sweaty palms and a shaky feeling in my insides, she admitted to herself.

"Can't you be more specific about what dinner on the grounds means. Sounds gross to me."

"It's just another name for an outdoor get-together after the service. A kind of picnic where everybody brings what they want, and we all spread our food together. St. Elisabeth's has one the third Sunday of every month. That's the one Sunday a preacher comes to the church to preach."

"Okay, so it's a picnic. But why on the ground? And why do we have to wait till dinner time?"

Dell laughed and shook his head. "To us Southerners, dinner means the noon meal. And grounds mean the church property. We'll start out in the church house. Do some singing. Listen to some preaching from Brother Rutherford. Maybe have a short business meeting after that. Then we get dismissed with prayer. That'll be about noon and then we go outside to spread our food on that table between the trees."

"Now I understand. 'All day singing and dinner on the grounds' explains it all, except to a dummy like me. It's really quite a sensible name."

"I think folks around here just think it's a perfectly ordinary name," Dell said, and grinned in his sexiest manner. "Gotcha that time, babe."

Cindi flashed a chiding look at him. Her eyelids at half-mast, she batted her feathery lashes at him till he grinned even more broadly. "You sure did," she said and put a whole new meaning in the three words.

"One thing about it, you'll be the prettiest girl there."

"And you'll be the best looking guy."

"I'll be the luckiest guy." Dell's words were flippant, but heart-felt. He meant every word. He could barely keep his attention on his driving. He wanted to stare at Cindi in her simple aqua dress with her laughing, open face that revealed her love for him along with every thought that passed through her head. Her mass of golden hair piled high on her head in a tumble of careless curls fascinated him, too. Making him want to plunge his hands through it as he drew her close. Good thing the trip in the truck would be short.

"Will I know anyone?" Cindi asked a little later as the truck pulled into the churchyard.

"Sure, me."

Cindi gave him a love pat for that remark. Then she pulled herself upright on the seat and moved away from him when she spotted Samantha Carver among the people milling everywhere. Relieved she would have someone to talk to besides Dell, she also hoped the woman hadn't seen Dell's arm around her shoulder. Much less that Cindi's head had been lying on his shoulder.

She also hoped she could control her telltale face so the woman wouldn't be able to see her change of attitude toward her. After hearing Dell's story of Cordelia's death, Cindi now understood the woman's problems. She ached with sympathy for her, but was afraid Samantha wouldn't want that.

"I didn't expect to see so many people here," she said. The churchyard was rapidly filling up with people of all ages. Most of the ladies wore soft summer dresses, fluttering long below their knees. Some wore broad-brimmed hats to defeat the sun's bright rays. Cindi looked down at her similar attire. A pale aqua cotton dress with a pleated broomstick skirt skimmed her body. The bodice had a modest neckline and showed off her tan. She'd chosen the dress for its comfort and coolness, sure to last through this "all day" affair. She admitted in her heart of hearts that it flattered her, and Dell might think she looked fetching in it.

"There are so many kids here," Cindi said next. In the crowd was a mob of children still neat and tidy from their parents' last minute grooming before they left home. As the kids darted everywhere through the grown-ups, Tai leaped from the truck to join them.

"Out here in the country, this is a big to-do for the little ones," Dell said, loving the way eyes softened at the sight of the children.

"You are the best looking guy here," Cindi affirmed after looking over the other men. All were dressed casually as Dell was in jeans and short sleeve shirts. None looked as great as Dell did to her love-charmed eyes, though.

"Just the luckiest, babe. And I want to stay that way, so don't look too hard at the other guys."

Just then Cindi burst out, "Jeff Carver, that big hypocrite, still looks as up-tight as ever." Jeff, with his spray net hair and ever-bristling mustache wore a long sleeved shirt that looked uncomfortably warm. His Dockers as usual were too perfectly pressed.

He wears long sleeved shirts to hide the needle marks. That chilling thought hit Cindi and a hard, involuntary rigor shook her frame. She hid her reaction as she saw Samantha hurrying over to them.

"We enjoyed meeting your friends, Cindi," Samantha said. Her light dress swished around her legs as she moved toward them. "The music was wonderful, too. Cordelia was sorry she didn't get to come with us, but I'll bring her over soon. You've just got to meet her."

I wonder what she'd say if I told her I already had. I wonder what she'd say if I asked her where her daughter is today.

But Cindi couldn't be that mean so she replied kindly to Samantha's unsettling remarks. "Please do come over to see me again soon."

In the bright heat of the summer morning, Cindi shivered again as creeping icy shudders clutched her mid-section. *Samantha is completely mental. Or maybe on drugs herself. Or maybe she knows Cordelia's spirit is unable to rest.* Cindi gave herself a shake to help the goose bumps subside.

Dell began unloading the lawn chairs and picnic basket from the truck. Samantha took Cindi around to introduce her to everyone. Soon Dell came to rescue her from the woman and escort her into the church house to find a seat for the singing.

CHAPTER 14

The small church wasn't air-conditioned. It didn't seem uncomfortably hot to Cindi. Ceiling fans kept the air stirring unlike that hot, still day when she and Dell and Tai sought shelter there from the summer storm. That day seemed aeons ago now, far removed by all the events that crowded between it and this one.

Cindi pushed her memories away and began to enjoy the singing. Though the simple melodies poured forth from untrained throats and were sung lustily with no finesse, Cindi gloried in the sound. Most of the songs were old, familiar hymns. Cindi found she was able to join in if she didn't use her full voice, but sang lightly instead.

After the congregational singing, a men's quartet sang several numbers a capella. Cindi marveled at their intricate harmonies and ability to stay true to pitch without any accompaniment. After they sang, the preacher gave a simple message about the love of God. Cindi found comfort in his words and the verses he read from the Bible.

She offered silent prayers for her father, once again begging he be returned to her alive. Brother Rutherford ended his sermon long before the hottest part of the day. The crowd exited into the churchyard, and swarmed around the eating tables drawing Cindi and Dell with them.

"Come on, everybody. It's time for the melon eating contest," Brother Rutherford announced after everyone had eaten dinner.

Ice-cold watermelons appeared, taken from their resting places deep in the crushed ice of thermal insulated chests. They were cut into slices and the contest got underway.

"I'm so stuffed with food, I'd rather go walk in the graveyard," Cindi told to Dell who had already declined participation in the contest.

"Let's go, then," Dell agreed. He turned away from her and gave a piercing whistle.

Tai, busy chasing sticks for some of the children, heard and ambled toward them with his usual dignity re-assumed. As the trio neared the newest grave, the one of Lonnie Benson, Tai gave a short, agitated "woof" as he had done the other time they walked here. This time Cindi noticed an unpleasant odor hanging like a miasma over the area. She ignored the smell since Dell was holding her hand as they walked. He was saying outrageous, almost unbelievable sweet nothings to her. She and Dell sauntered on, but Tai stayed behind, snuffling and pawing at the grave.

At last, her face flushed and warmth burning in her cheeks and spreading to the rest of her body, Cindi warned Dell, "We'll have to leave this polite company soon if you don't stop making these scandalous, exciting remarks to me."

Dell's reply was swallowed up in Tai's sudden outburst of frenzied barking. Cindi gave a glance over her shoulder and met Tai's agitated, pleading stare. His distress was apparent. Cindi gave Dell's arm a shake then made him look at Tai, too. The dog was digging earnestly at the grave, throwing clods of red dirt behind him as he dug. Cindi and Dell could hear him barking louder and faster. He had taken Cindi's attention to him as encouragement.

"You'll have to go back and get Tai, Dell," she said. "He won't quit digging at that grave. He's going to get in trouble."

Dell tried whistling and calling, but Tai ignored him and continued to dig and bark. A small crowd gathered around the dog. Dell went to the truck for a leash.

Approaching the grave, Cindi saw Tai pull on something. Cindi drew close enough to see what Tai had unearthed and gasped. With horror she recognized a human arm wearing a jagged red sleeve. At first she thought Tai had dug up Lonnie Benson.

Dell slipped the leash on Tai and led him away. The sleeved arm lay exposed on the disturbed earth of the grave. Cindi glimpsed something bulkier under the disturbed soil. She couldn't tear her horrified gaze away. She could tell the arm belonged to a woman. One slim red-nailed finger still wore a very large emerald ring. Cindi feared she knew who was buried with Lonnie Benson.

Dell returned and gave support to her hunch. "Miss Flowers," he cried in an anguished voice. Just the sight of the hand brought recognition. Tai's howling from the truck added to the horrific moment. Cindi walked over to the dog and quieted his howls till they turned to heart-broken whimpers.

The rest of the time at St. Elisabeth's passed in a blur for Cindi. She and Samantha along with the rest of the women retreated to shade of the oak trees by the food table. They busied themselves stowing leftovers into containers and picnic baskets. They tidied up the eating area and folded up the additional tables and lawn chairs.

One lady corralled the children into a group and took them back into the church. Cindi could hear their young voices singing and then the lady's voice as she told them Bible stories to keep them distracted from the activities in the graveyard.

Dell and the other men stood around the grave. A deputy sheriff there for the day's events called his superiors.

Cindi and Dell stayed until more officials arrived. Dell confirmed the identity of the corpse to the officials, basing his confirmation on her distinctive ring and the appearance of her hand. The decomposing condition of the body made identification difficult and hid the cause of death.

"She always wore it," he said. "I never saw her without it."

One of the deputies questioned him briefly, and promised to come to Magnolia House for a full statement later. Cindi knew she must tell what she knew of Consuelo's proposed trip to Colombia and later disappearance. As she and Dell headed for home, they discussed exactly what they would tell the officials.

Later that afternoon when the same deputy sheriff's car pulled up in front of Magnolia House, Cindi walked out to greet him. The man was a perfect picture of authority in his well-pressed khaki uniform with his holstered gun resting on his lean hip. Incredibly tall, he stood ramrod straight. His face was shadowed by a peaked straw hat, while his mirrored sunglasses hid the expression in his eyes.

"I've been expecting you," Cindi said, her own face vulnerable to his gaze. "Dell Comeaux is mowing grass out back. I'll signal him to come and answer your questions."

"Thanks." The deputy removed his hat respectfully and introduced himself. "My name is Bud Morgan. I've been assigned to this case. And you are?"

"Cindi Lynn, I'm Jim Lynn's daughter. Miss Flowers asked me to housesit for her while she went to South America. Colombia, more specifically. It's a long story." Cindi still felt nervous, but the man's quiet dignity and kind manner calmed her a little. Her voice trembled as she added, "I don't really know the lady, but I was with Dell when her body was found."

"Just take your time and tell me about it in your own way. I'll ask questions if I need to." The officer's voice was firm and polite. It gave Cindi confidence.

They reached the rear deck. Cindi signaled to Dell. While they waited for him to come, she explained how she happened to come to Magnolia House. "I wonder if I should stay on now. Who will the house belong to?" she finished.

"Your father of course," Dell said, arriving in time to hear her last words. "You've got to stay. He wants you to." Then Dell began by giving his version of how Tai had dug up the body. He went on to tell the deputy about Rita and Cliff, and told some of the conversation he had overheard in the woods. That damning conversation that suggested their implication in Consuelo Flowers' death.

Dell also told the lawman about Cliff's mention of the shipment that required Rita to stay an extra day at Magnolia House. He told the deputy his suspicions about smuggling activities at the Carver airstrip.

"You should have told all this to us when you learned of it, Dell. After all, I remember you working for us at the office while you were still in high school. You used to sweep up and keep the place clean, didn't you? You, of all people, should know we need the cooperation of every honest citizen. The shipment might be illegal drugs or some other contraband."

"I'm sorry I didn't tip you off."

"We'll have to get a warrant to conduct a search of Carver's business. Just let us know if anything else suspicious happens," Deputy Morgan said. "We've taken Miss Flowers' body to the morgue in Shreveport. If we find she was murdered, we'll probably pull Mr. Aymond in for questioning. I suppose I don't need to add that I'd prefer you don't talk about anything we've discussed this afternoon with anyone else. I'm not sure we could extradite Mr. Aymond from South America if he got spooked and ran."

The officer got in to his patrol car and left; Cindi drew a deep breath and collapsed in Dell's arms. So now the police knew everything she and Dell knew. Or did they? Well, they knew everything about Rita and Cliff. Somehow, neither she nor Dell had talked about any of the scary things that had been happening around Magnolia House or the emeralds.

* * *

Cindi found the days following the horrifying discovery at St. Elisabeth's were passing in a quiet enchantment. Nights, and sometimes days, were spent in passionate lovemaking with Dell. Her own abandon surprised her, but she let her love for him control her. Alone on the estate, the lovers didn't hesitate to follow their hearts and made love whenever and wherever they wanted to.

She marveled anew over their growing relationship. Dell spent his nights in Magnolia House now, in the mirrored bedroom where Cindi slept. Each night was filled with closeness and passion. Dell made her feel safe and protected all through the night. When she roused from sleep during the dark hours, just the soft sound of his even breathing soothed her.

"Dell," Cindi murmured drowsily one morning as she woke up. More loudly, she added "Sweetheart?" Eyes only half open, her searching hands failed to encounter his lithe, muscular body. She realized he must have already gotten up.

She opened her eyes and saw the bedside clock. "Drat, I've overslept as usual. He's probably already in the kitchen." She stretched sensuously and thoughts of their previous night's lovemaking crowded her mind. A rosy flush heated her face and limbs.

"Come on, girl," Dell called from the bathroom door. "It's time for your bath."

Cindi looked at him, and smiled. "I guess you heard me talking to myself. I thought you were already in the kitchen. Yes, a bath before breakfast would be nice."

Dell stretched out his hand to her. "I guess you're entitled to talk to yourself. You have to make up for all the time your throat wouldn't let you talk much."

Cindi laughed and jumped from the bed to join him. She sang a few bars as she went to join him. The air of the bathroom was scented with Cindi's favorite lemony bubble bath.

"Come on in," Dell said. "The water's fine. It will make you feel divine."

Cindy chuckled, remembering their afternoon in the pool just a short time ago.

"This scent is perfect for Magnolia House," she said as she joined him among the bubbles. "Maybe that's another reason I like it so much here. I've always loved that smell."

"The blooms are almost finished. You'll have to depend on the bubble bath to tide you through till next year."

Next year? Did he expect her to stay? Could she stay? Consuelo who had given her permission to do so was dead.

She wouldn't ask. Instead she said, "Things have been so quiet here lately. Ever since the dinner on the grounds." She turned around and traced Dell's eyebrows with a lazy finger leaving a trail of soapsuds behind.

Dell grabbed a handful of suds and gave her a dripping beard in retaliation. "That was excitement enough to last me a lifetime," he said. He added a soapy mustache to her face. "Maybe two lifetimes. Maybe excitement isn't the right word either. I guess I mean terribleness, sadness, even horribleness, instead."

Cindi nodded. "I never even knew Consuelo, but now I wish I had," she said, as she added a beard to his face. They sat facing each other in the huge whirlpool tub of the master bath, legs entangled in the frothing water. "I can't even hate her any more. And her part in Father's leaving us doesn't even matter to me now. Do you miss her, Dell? I never knew her, and I'm grieving for her. Whenever I sit down to play, the saddest tunes come out."

"Sure I miss her. I grieve for her. But you make me so happy, even sadness for her loss doesn't reach my soul. Ma'am, would you please come closer? My babe, my *querida.*" He stretched out his arms and drew her to his smooth, muscled chest. He kissed her soapy face repeatedly. The steamy mist rising from the water enveloped them. The water made their bodies slippery, made them slide against each other. The eased friction gave such a different sensation, Cindi felt her passion spiral higher than ever.

She lay contentedly against Dell, the excitement fizzing between them, but comforting her as well.

"Querida, you are desired," he whispered.

"Someday you're going to tell me exactly what that word means."

"Q*uerida,* is that the word you mean*?* I think it means darling, dearest, or something like that. My folks practice their Spanish often. You know, for their missionary trips to Mexico. *Querida* is what my father calls my mother. It's the one thing I approve of about my parents. They've taught me how married people can keep love alive. They truly love each other."

Cindi wanted to ask Dell if that meant he loved her, perhaps wanted to build a life with her, but as she gathered her courage, he turned her gently until her back was to him. The sensations this position caused robbed her of speech. She leaned back against his muscled torso. The soft mat of his chest hair cushioned her as his hands cupped her breasts. His thumbs flicked her nipples until they hardened to an aching peak. His mouth moved over the back of her neck.

She was melting. She was molten liquid. She would slip out with the recirculating water of the tub. But Dell would not let her go. His hands moved down further and cupped her buttocks, kneading and stroking them. She felt the hard shaft of him against her soft curves. She could bear no more.

She struggled to turn toward him. "Please, Dell. I need to touch you, kiss you."

He turned her toward him with his strong hands. He lifted her body, then entered her and settled her against him in a smooth, continuous movement. It was so swift, it took Cindi's breath away.

Their bodies pulsed together. The sensations built higher as they surged toward fulfillment. When the climax came, it was explosive, lifting them to another time, another plane. They lay spent together in the afterglow of their lovemaking, their limbs all tangled in the warm, moving water and steamy moist air. The light, flowery scent of Cindi's bubble bath, the susurration of the water as it roiled in the tub all were a part of the enchantment surrounding them.

Cindi raised her head from Dell's chest. The sunshine from the skylight glinted on the water and she narrowed her eyes against the glare. She gazed at Dell's face, drinking in the sight of him. His breathing was slow and even, his eyes closed. Had he gone back to sleep?

She stirred and tried to rise. His quick grin startled her as he pulled her back down. "Gotcha, babe," he declared. "And just where did you think you were going?"

Cindi felt his member stirring and hardening against her. Her own desire returned. The lovers began again their quest for fulfillment.

*   *   *

Later as Cindi dressed for the day, she wondered how she could even think of returning to the West Coast. Her throat was well, her sorrow for her mother eased. Yet how could she leave even if the sheriff's department would allow her to?

She couldn't. Not feeling as she did for Dell. Though what she hoped for and expected from him, she couldn't really say. She must stay also, because Consuelo and her father had asked her to. She shrugged off her bothersome thoughts and planned the rest of her day.

"Woof?" Tai stood in the doorway between the bedroom and sitting room. The dog never rested easily in the confines of Magnolia House, but he slept in the sitting room of the master suite each night now. He refused to move any farther into the house than the doorway of her room. He claimed the rug before the fireplace in the sitting room as his bed.

Cindi padded over to open the door to the patio so Tai could go outside. She murmured soft words of praise to her canine protector as he slipped outside.

The dog's restless movements during the nights were the only unusual nocturnal sounds of late. There were no other disturbances. The spirits and ghostly apparitions had taken a holiday or left with Rita. No unearthly cries or shouts sounded. The panther ceased prowling in the atrium. The respite was welcome.

Cindi went to the kitchen to prepare breakfast. She put the finishing touches to *chocolate santafarena* and *tostados de maiz*. Though Rita was gone, the menus she'd used were firmly in place. Cindi laid the beautiful rose pottery dishes out to place on their breakfast trays. She hummed happily and occasionally burst into short snatches of song.

Dell's going to be so pleased. I think I've really gotten the hang of these dishes. I hope he's worked up a good appetite. Pleased with herself, she continued to work.

Soundlessly Dell approached. He spied shamelessly on her, letting her mood take over his own, as he reveled in the sight of her. Her long, white-blonde hair hung loose this morning. Still damp from their bath time, it curled where it willed, riotously clustering around her rosy, beaming face. He began to plan a second painting of her as she appeared at that moment.

He made himself known to her by seizing her shoulders gently and nuzzling her neck. His attentions brought her head arching back, and a contented smile to her lips.

After breakfast as she and Dell lingered over coffee, Cindi told Dell her plans for the day. "Summer's passing. Fall's coming. I'm going to start some fall cleaning this morning. I'm sure the house needs a thorough scrubbing so that's what I'm going to do. I've never really looked into every nook and cranny on the second floor, so that's where I'll start."

"I've got some finishing touches to add to your portrait, so don't count on me to help," Dell demurred. "You just get right to your house cleaning. I'll whip up something for us to eat when I get through painting."

Cindi climbed the stairs to begin the task she had set for herself. In the second story bedrooms and baths, she discovered unique features her father had placed everywhere. Whimsical touches that hadn't shown up on those blueprints she'd once studied. A stained glass window high up in the wall at the end of the balcony, fanciful animal spigots and more stained glass windows in the baths. Not to mention a loft in one of the bedrooms only reached by climbing a ladder like one found in a ship.

What a perfect room for a child. Had her father been thinking of her when he designed it? For a moment she let herself imagine a little tow-headed girl or perhaps a little boy about four or five with Dell's strong features and curly brown hair. Her heart yearned for the tots she'd conjured up.

As she cleaned the balcony, she pictured the little girl with her cotton top hair wisping around her face. She saw the child playing with her dolls spread everywhere on the balcony. The sturdy, curly-headed boy drove toy cars on the railings, making engine noises. The images of the children burned into her consciousness as she continued her mundane housecleaning jobs.

Any child would love living and playing in this house. Especially in that bedroom with the loft, or on the upstairs balcony, or among the thriving plants downstairs in the garden room. The house cried out for a family to fill its many rooms. Cindi wondered if her father had ever felt the same way.

As she kept up her busy work, an expectant joy welled up as if she were preparing the house for some arrival. She found pleasure in cleaning windows and scrubbing baseboards and walls. She energetically took down curtains, carrying them to the laundry room to wash.

In Rita's room, she cleaned with great care. Alert, she looked for some clue to the woman's destination when she left Magnolia House. She justified her actions because Rita might also be the victim of foul play. If so, any clue might lead to her whereabouts…or her body.

Rita had never been her favorite person, still Cindi found herself hoping she would turn up alive somewhere. Perhaps she would breeze in some day as if she had never left. Spouting Spanish with every breath, and setting up a clamor with the pots in the kitchen as she cooked, Rita's return would bring Cindi relief.

Most of Rita's loose daytime garments were still hanging in her closet. Cindi couldn't decide what might be missing, other than her flaming red nightwear. Either Rita left thinking she would only be gone overnight, or she left behind the discarded clothing she had used to play the role of a servant. Cindi found boxes in the utility room and packed away Rita's abandoned garments and belongings.

After a thorough cleaning of the second floor rooms was completed, Cindi turned her attention to the balcony overlooking the atrium and lower halls. She was vacuuming there when the idea struck her. Standing exactly where she had seen Rita the night they sighted the panther, she gripped the rail much as Rita had done and stared down.

Something was wrong. This spot was directly in front of Rita's room, but something about the view from that vantage point stirred an elusive, uneasy remembrance. In vain, Cindi struggled to recall the errant scrap of memory.

Giving up, she started another task. Vacuuming the stairs with a portable cleaner, she carefully went over each step. She expected at any moment to have another front panel fall open before her. But no other hidden cubbyhole turned up. She searched the one that had held the emeralds. She looked carefully for any other treasure or clue, but all in vain. It was empty.

Cindi ignored the smells and the accompanying sounds of activity from downstairs in the kitchen as long as possible. Wonderful aromas told of Dell's presence there. Her stomach rumbled in response. She traipsed downstairs, going first to the laundry to check on the curtains.

"How long till supper?" She called to signal her presence.

"It's nearly ready."

"Whatever you're fixing smells wonderful. Let me dash upstairs and re-hang these curtains. I'll be right back."

Fifteen minutes or so later, Dell heard her footsteps coming down the circular den stairs. "I've got to go to Shreveport on business tomorrow," he called out to her. "If you drove your rental car in, and dropped it off at the airport, I might be persuaded to pick you up there and take you out for dining and dancing."

"Umm, sounds good. Just what we need, a night out," she whispered in his ear though she had to tiptoe to do so. She didn't stop with words, but flicked her tongue lightly over his ear lobe and twined her fingers through his rumpled hair. This suggestion of his was her first hint that Dell wasn't expecting her to be flying away to California either.

"Stop that. These veal cutlets will be burnt if you don't back off," he muttered. "I don't attack you when you're cooking."

"You don't have to. I don't need any help to burn what I cook. Besides, you can't call this an attack. I just whispered softly in your ear, and gave that ear a little extra attention." Cindi dropped down flat footed and stepped away nonetheless, the better to stare at him. He was flushed from the heat of the stove. His hair curled wildly from the steam. He was beautiful.

"You're getting better at cooking all the time," he said in a consoling tone.

"Get serious, Dell. I've got a long way to go before I'm near as good as you." As she talked, she took out dishes to set the table. "I've got something to ask you. Remember those sketches Rita showed us when she first came? You remember. My father had drawn them and written funny comments on them. They looked like they were all of the same woman. A woman who looked like Rita."

Dell nodded, and continued stirring the gravy he was now busy with.

Cindi, satisfied that he knew what she was talking about, went on. "When Miss Marie was here, she found something had been erased on one of them. The word looked like prim. I just thought Father was making a comment about the woman."

"Prim, huh? Once upon a time I used to think that word described you. But that was before I ever saw you," he interjected.

Cindi blushed and shook her head. "Oh sure. Well, I once upon a time thought prim was a word that fit me, too. Getting back to Miss Marie, she looked carefully at the sketch with her glasses. The letters e-r-a had once been part of the end of the word. Miss Marie says *primera* means first cousin in Spanish. She and I wondered if that meant Rita was Consuelo's first cousin."

"I guess that would explain quite a few things that have been bugging me," Dell said. He turned the heat off under the gravy and prepared to serve their meal. "For instance, how could she afford such expensive lingerie."

Cindi who was offering the plate to him to fill with food, felt a sudden urge to throw one at him instead. Trust a man to remember Rita's distinctive nighties.

"Oh you," she said in disgust. "I was thinking more along the lines of her musical training. It was evident when she played for us the night she disappeared. So this morning on the balcony, I realized she certainly had the skill to be the one who played *Claire de Lune* for me the first night she spent in the house. Besides that, I realized that she walked up to me from the wrong direction that night. She approached me as if she had come down the stairs to the den instead of the ones that end in the front hall. So that means she was probably already downstairs before I screamed."

"What are you getting at? Are you saying you think she played the piano that night?"

"Yes, I guess that's about it. I just don't know how she managed the disappearing act at the end or why there was blood on the keys. Maybe she pricked her finger on the little piano that was left on the Steinway. She probably was behind most of the strange things happening around here. I'm sure she snooped in my rooms and moved my clothes around."

"She probably wanted to borrow some of your stuff. Something that might make her look as great as you always do."

"That's not what I meant at all."

"Do you really think she's behind some of the scary things that have happened? We'll call Deputy Morgan later and tell him. For now, soup's on, let's eat. The food will energize our brains and give us lots of zip for later on."

After their meal, Dell asked Cindi if she wanted to hike to the church with him. It would be their first venture back there.

Cindi felt a strange compulsion to continue her housework, but she agreed to go with him. There seemed to be some reason she must get it done as soon as possible.

They found the woods dusty and dry now. Even the pine trees looked dull and their aroma was muted instead of sharp. The few wild flowers left bloomed defiantly in spite of the heat. Many had wilted and left dried stalks standing where they once flowered, bringing beauty to the landscape.

Though the worst heat of the hot Louisiana summer day had passed at this late hour, it was still quite warm. Cindi and Dell walked slowly on the dusty path. They walked side-by-side for the path was narrow. Cindi's arm circled Dell's waist, Dell kept his hand lightly, but in a possessive way, on the nape of Cindi's neck. Tai moved slowly at their heels, panting heavily from the effort.

"We probably should have waited till early in the morning to do this," Dell said. "I had forgotten how warm it would be. It's just that tomorrow is going to be a full day. My appointment is at one. What time do you want me to pick you up at the airport?"

"I'll clean the downstairs of the house tomorrow morning. Then I'll get ready and can probably be there by five o'clock."

Dell explained the route she should follow to Shreveport and how to get to the airport as they continued their trek to the church.

When they came to Loggy Branch, the water no longer rippled within the banks. Instead, it seeped along slowly in a scanty trickle. Even at the crossing, they hardly needed the stepping stones. Tai made full use of them though, bounding from one to the other.

"Somebody else has been here," Dell noted as he pointed to heavy marks in the drying mud alongside the stones and on the other side of the stream. "Looks like the tracks of a large animal, plus somebody's footprints."

"Yes, and the animal didn't waste time on the stepping stones," Cindi observed. "The footprints are so small," she added. Her forehead wrinkled in thought. She and Dell looked at each other, the same idea striking both of them at the identical time.

"Rita," Cindi said.

"The Loggy Branch monster," Dell said.

"And it looks as if the cat was stalking her."

"Could be." Dell moved closer to examine the prints. Cindi stood panic-stricken as he moved away from her.

"Oh no," she said. "Rita was always terrified of the panther. I wonder if a phantom panther could really hurt a real live person."

"Probably so, the phantom could scare a real live person to death."

Cindi and Dell kept their eyes open for any other signs of Rita or the phantom panther. If there were any, they failed to spot them.

Once at the church, Dell headed for Consuelo's recent resting place. "Since we're here, I want to visit Lonnie Benson's grave. Call it morbid curiosity if you like, but I've got to see with my own eyes that things are back the way they should be."

"I guess it's only natural for you to feel that way," Cindi agreed. "Maybe it's a fascination or compulsion, but I feel it, too." Suddenly she couldn't get the sight of the woman's lifeless arm out of her mind. The image of that arm, and especially that one elegant, red-nailed finger with the beautiful emerald ring filled her brain, causing it to whirl maddeningly. For a moment she imagined the red dirt was still disturbed, the corpse still half-exposed.

She blinked and the image vanished. The dirt was no longer disturbed, the cemetery was orderly once more. Lonnie Benson's casket had been decently covered again and the earth was smooth and unbroken over it. Someone had even placed a tombstone on the grave to replace the temporary cardboard one.

Who is Lonnie Benson? Dell told me he was the last of his family. Cindi expelled the breath she'd been holding. Dell, walking at her side, seemed unaware of her distress and subsequent relief.

They walked on. Dell paused when they came to Cordelia's marker. Cindi almost spoke of seeing the ghost she believed to be her. She couldn't do it.

"You know only the physical bodies of those who've left this plane are here. Gradually those remains decay and return to the earth," she managed to say. She stared at the smooth gray gravestone, then bent to pick at a greenish lichen patch marring its surface. "Their spirits are not here. They've gone on." She stopped, not knowing what to say next.

"I wish I knew Cordelia's spirit had gone and was at peace. She deserves that."

"We don't know for sure that it's Cordelia who cries the panther's name and walks at Magnolia House," Cindi objected, all the while believing with certainty that it assuredly was.

Dell, Cindi and Tai made the return trip to the Flowers property. As the two walked slowly back up the slope to the house, they saw a sheriff's car parked in the driveway. Deputy Morgan lounged against the fender of the cruiser. He waved and called to them, saying he'd just driven up.

"I'm glad you've come," Cindi said. "I just thought of some things you might find interesting."

"And we've found footprints near Loggy Branch that could have been made by Rita Gomez," Dell added. "We also found some animal tracks. I think they're painter tracks." Dell purposefully used the local word.

"I'd like to see the prints after Miss Lynn tells me about these interesting things she remembered," said Deputy Morgan.

"Please come in. I have some sketches to show you. My father drew them and they resemble Rita Gomez. She came here claiming to have worked for my father, and she may have done that, but I believe she was related to Consuelo as well."

Cindi went to her room for the sketch. While she was gone, Dell told officer some of the things that had been happening around the house. Haunting episodes that had escalated since Cindi's arrival.

When Cindi returned with the sketch to show Morgan, she told her version of the eerie happenings. She began with her peripheral vision of the panther the night she arrived. Cordelia's appearance on the deck during the party was the only thing she omitted. She wanted to tell Dell first.

"Do you believe that Ms. Gomez and/or Mr. Aymond somehow arranged all these strange things?" Morgan asked.

"Maybe, I'm not sure. Even if they did create the moonlight piano serenade, I'm not sure they did all of the other things." Cindi knew she sounded like a complete idiot, contradicting herself at every turn.

Dell added his opinion of the strange occurrences. "I don't think they're responsible for everything either. After all, people have been seeing the panther long before now." He didn't add he was one of those people. Then he changed the subject by asking, "Are your people any closer to figuring out anything about Miss Flowers' death?"

"Not really," the deputy answered. "I came by today because I wanted to talk to you about the phone call you received from her, Miss Lynn. Do you remember exactly when you got that call? I mean date and time to the minute."

Cindi thought back. "It was the day of my mother's funeral, so it was June fourteenth. It was late in the day out on the West Coast. I think about eight o'clock probably. It wasn't dark yet."

"We think she could have been killed shortly afterward. The cause of death was a blow to the head. There were also marks around her throat indicating someone tried to strangle her. She may have called you just minutes before she died. Perhaps the killer was with her when she made the call. Did you hear any other voice in the background, or any noise?"

"It's just too long ago to be certain but I really don't think so," Cindi said, shaking her head for emphasis.

"Dell, is there anything else you remember about the day Miss Flowers left?"

"I didn't actually see her leave," Dell said. "She sent me to Ida on an errand. I took the house key to the FedEx guy to send to Cindi. When I got back, Miss Flowers' car was gone."

"And that would be the silver Porsche we found at the airport?"

"Yes, that's the car."

"Perhaps I shouldn't tell you this," Deputy Morgan said. "But since you tipped us off where to look, I will. We've found evidence that smuggling activities have indeed been going on at the Carver airstrip. Illegal drugs and aliens have been coming in there."

Dell looked shocked. "Aliens? Little green men?"

Deputy Morgan laughed. "Illegal aliens as in people without authority to come into this country. Colombians and Mexicans without visas, not weird space aliens."

Dell's face assumed a satisfied look. "That explains a lot of things," he said. "I was pretty sure they were bringing in drugs. That's how Jeff Carver got his supply. But people as well, I wasn't sure about that. I think Miss Flowers was in on that part. I wouldn't be talking about this to any other law officer, but somehow I trust you."

"You wouldn't be accusing any of my fellow officers of wrong doing, would you?"

"Take it whatever way you want to. It's always seemed strange to me that Jeff could continue to deal drugs and never get caught." He didn't mention his suspicions about Jeff having Cordelia's autopsy report changed. He'd said enough.

The deputy looked as if he would like to refute Dell's accusation, instead he said, "Let's go look at those tracks. I won't let anything you've said about Mr. Carver or Miss Flowers go any farther. At least for the time being."

As the two men walked off, Cindi wavered between fear that Dell might not be safe alone with the deputy, and belief in Deputy Morgan's integrity. She was glad for once Tai had left her side to follow Dell.

CHAPTER 15

"Eating dinner on the deck is great. I really enjoy it," Dell said as the gentle south breeze lifted and tousled his long brown hair. "Having you here to share the food with is great, too. You've done an excellent job with dinner today, babe."

"It's your turn tomorrow. I'm requesting one of your Tex-Mex omelets, please."

"Sure, babe." The two sat side by side. Dell gave her free hand a squeeze as he marveled to himself how things had changed between them since their first breakfast in this place. "Tex-Mex omelets tomorrow for breakfast. Say, what was the time you are getting to the airport, sweetheart?"

Cindi used her other hand to bring her napkin up to her lips, hiding a smile at her lover's nervousness. Dell's chitchat about meals and breakfast betrayed it. She just wished he'd get so caught up in his nervous chatter he'd tell her what his business trip to Shreveport was all about. She was pretty sure that wasn't going to happen, though.

"Dell, you've already asked me that at least twice this evening, not to mention at least once yesterday," Cindi said. "Every time I've told you the same thing. I'll try to be there at 5 P.M. Are you going to tell me anything about this mysterious appointment? It must be very important to put you in such a sweat."

"It's not making me sweat. And the answer to your question is easy. No. Call me superstitious or something. I'm afraid to talk about it."

"Okay. We won't talk about it."

Dell appeared relieved. "Cindi, you know you don't have to worry about getting lost on your way to Shreveport. You've been to Ida quite a few times with me. Once you get to Ida, just head south. That means a right turn on Highway 71. Then you just stay on that highway until you see the 220 exit after you've gotten to Shreveport."

Cindi shook her head. She couldn't believe her ears. He'd only given her the directions three times already. She finally cut him short. "Did I even once mention I was afraid of getting lost on the way to the airport? I don't think so. I think you've explained my route thoroughly. Besides, when I made a wrong turn—not got lost—on the way here from the airport, it was getting dark, and I was tired and—get the picture?"

"Hey, babe, forgive me."

He looked so contrite and so earnest, Cindi reached over to kiss him. "Sure," she whispered.

* * *

Much later Cindi lay sleepless. By now she was as nervous as Dell seemed to be over the trip to Shreveport. She really wanted to know what was going on. She also wondered where he planned to take her for dinner tomorrow night. When she dared to ask after they'd made love, he only told her to look gorgeous and plan to dance all night.

She wished she could get up and start the cleaning she still had to do. Some strange compulsion to get the whole place spotless was growing minute by minute. She'd have to wait till morning. She didn't want to wake Dell.

Dell lay sleepless as well. His mind was full of the extra places he planned to visit before and after his appointment. He had a few stops to make before he met Cindi. Just which stops depended on the outcome of his appointment. He didn't want Cindi to have a clue either.

"Please bear with me, sweetheart," he said as he took Cindi in his arms the next morning for a last kiss and hug. "Believe me, you'll be glad you waited to find out."

"Dell, I'll wait, but if we keep on kissing and hugging, you probably won't even leave, much less meet me at the airport."

After several more kisses and caresses, Dell left. Almost as soon as he backed the pickup out of the garage, Cindi was once more hard at work on the house.

She focused her energy on the first floor. None of the formal rooms needed more than a thorough vacuuming and dusting. She remembered how beautiful the rooms looked during the musicale. Then they were filled with people and flowers the way they deserved to be. They always would be if she lived here. What was she thinking of? So far there had been no clue on the ownership of Magnolia House now Consuelo was gone.

Had Consuelo left a will? Was her father the heir? If so, with Louisiana's forced heirship—a law based on the Napoleonic Code—the house might belong to her.

Soon Cindi was through with everything but the rooms she'd been using. As she carefully dusted Consuelo's piano collection, she tried to imagine places that might conceal hidden cubbyholes. If there were any more hiding places, these rooms had many likely looking spots where they could be concealed. She wasn't at all sure what she was looking for. She only knew there was something she must find.

When she made her first discovery, she was elated. It was a securely locked safe behind the cabinet where the miniature pianos were displayed. It was cleverly concealed yet in plain view. Set carefully in a *trompe l'oeil* panel that mimicked real plants so perfectly, Cindi tried to water them before she noticed the difference.

"I should have known these weren't real plants. By now they would have turned into dry brown stalks," Cindi told Tai who lounged on the sitting room rug. Her voice held such excitement, Tai barked in response.

Idly she twirled the dial trying to open the safe. Of course she had no idea as to the combination. All her best efforts to discover the right numbers failed. She couldn't imagine what richer treasure than the emeralds she'd already found might be hidden in the safe. She gave up trying to open it.

Then as she dusted the shelves, she noticed an empty spot on one of the shelves. Could one of the pianos be missing? She found another empty spot. Two were missing. Cindi couldn't believe it. The last time she had really looked at the shelves and the piano collection was while Miss Marie had been at the house. She was sure all of them had been on the shelves then. Maybe other things were missing as well.

Earlier, a cubbyhole in Consuelo's built-in desk had come to Cindi's attention. It contained the lady's personal journal and some letters from Colombia addressed in Jim Lynn's distinctive handwriting. Cindi had stuffed the pouch of emeralds behind the journal, sure no one but Consuelo would ever look there. She checked now. The book and letters were there. The pouch wasn't.

Cindi rummaged trough the small space, and saw a folded edge of paper sticking out of the diary. Hesitating only moments before paging through until she came to it, she found an envelope bearing her name. The letter she removed from the envelope began:

My dear child,

Since you've found this letter, it must be that I am no longer in the land of the living. I hope you've been able to keep Cliff and my cousin, Rita Gomez, from finding any of my treasures, or looting the ones I keep on open display in my own rooms.

I believe your father is still alive. He is a captive in Colombia. It is my intention to go there and secure his release as you know. Perhaps even though I have been stopped from doing so, he will escape on his own . Wait for him at Magnolia House.

Bring judgment to the ones who have killed me, Cliff Aymond, and his accomplice, Rita Gomez. Trust Dell Comeaux. He will help you bring down Cliff and Rita. Don't fear the panther, sometimes called Delia, or the ghost, Cordelia.

Lovingly, Consuelo Flowers

Cindi's hands quivered and trembled as she saw her suspicions confirmed by Consuelo's written testimony. But the letter raised as many questions as it answered. Why must the house be protected? How was Cindi's presence here supposed to do this?

It hadn't worked. Cindi knew she had already failed miserably. The emeralds and some of the tiny, jeweled pianos were missing. Rita had surely taken them with her.

Consuelo had told her not to fear the panther or Cordelia's ghost. Just saying the words over again out loud brought goose bumps to Cindi's arms. The fact that she was alone at the house gave an eerie feeling.

Trying to dispel her fear, and thinking of the puzzles revealed in the letter, Cindi began straightening the walk-in closet. Her own things took up only a small space there, but Consuelo's clothes crowded the closet. Cindi had seldom seen such a gorgeous array of apparel. What would become of all these beautiful garments now their owner was no more?

Cindi pouted all over again as she remembered Dell's answer when she asked him how to dress for their date. She looked over her meager wardrobe carefully, trying to decide on something she could wear. Dell had seen her in everything she had.

Consuelo's clothes were all too long for her, but maybe, just maybe, she could improvise something spectacular out of one of the woman's garments. She had a feeling Consuelo would be glad for Cindi to wear something of hers.

Thoughtfully she removed an ivory polished cotton pleated skirt from its hanger. It would almost reach her ankles, but she could wear it with the sweater she had worn for the musicale. It would swish in a satisfying fashion when she and Dell danced. That would do for tonight.

Cindi continued looking through the clothing. She saw other things she could shorten and wear. She decided to try her hand at the task. For instance, this over-sized peach shirt might make a long tunic for Cindi. Maybe she would wear it tonight instead of the sweater.

She needed a belt or sash though. She'd seen a sewing machine in one of the upstairs bedrooms. She thought she could fashion a sash easily and quickly from a colorful scarf she found. Her focus shifted from housecleaning to sewing as she headed upstairs.

Once at the machine, she couldn't find a pair of scissors.

She shook her head, muttering. "Why would anyone have such a lovely sewing machine and no scissors?" Annoyed, she remembered seeing scissors over at Dell's. In a flash she was down the stairs, and on her way to his little house.

He wouldn't mind her going into his place she was sure. After all, she was trying to look nice for him. The door was unlocked as he always left it. Dell's private space looked emptier than usual. Glancing around she slowly realized many of the pictures she was used to seeing on the walls were gone. The stacks piled around the room were smaller. She shrugged and went toward the drawer in the tiny kitchenette where she'd seen Dell store his scissors.

After she got them, the covered easel caught her eye. She hesitated, tempted to remove the cloth that covered her painting. She knew she shouldn't, but her curiosity was very strong. He'd captured her little girl self so perfectly, what had he done this time? Before she could stop herself, she pulled the cloth away.

She stared in awe. This curvaceous, half-clothed woman couldn't be her. Her eyes widened and a scowl creased her brow. What was this?

This painting was of a woman sprawled in a lounge chair on the patio outside the master bedroom. The woman wore a California Angels baseball cap and a hot pink bikini bottom. She'd posed for Dell fully clothed here in the pool house. Outrage and embarrassment heated her cheeks. Anger blazed in her eyes.

"He spied on me," she cried. "He was there on the patio while I slept. He saw my breasts then before I…that is we…uh." Her voice trailed away into an anguished squeal. She was unable to finish the sentence even to herself.

Staring at the portrait, she recognized the pose as the one Dell had arranged her in. This was the painting he'd been working on. The painting he kept telling her hadn't been finished. Cindi felt betrayed. It looked finished to her. She burst into tears. All the time he'd been fooling her, taking advantage of her. Maybe even making fun of her. No wonder he'd said nothing of love.

"I look as fat and hideous as one of those women those old Europeans painted. Ooh… I'm so mad. Who were those old guys? Rubens? Van Gogh?"

Tai whined uneasily. He'd followed her over to Dell's. Cindi sat down on the floor. She cuddled Tai in her arms for comfort.

"It looks like Dell's just been using me. He took advantage of me, Tai. He knew I would never let him paint me like this," she sobbed. "All he wanted was to show everyone how ugly and big I am."

"Ah, but you're not, Cindi, love. You have a most appealing womanly figure. The young man captured it perfectly."

She jumped up and whirled around to confront Cliff who was staring avidly at the exposed painting, as Tai bristled and growled at her side. "What are you doing here? I thought you were in Baton Rouge. And where is Rita? We haven't seen her for days. What have you done with her? Killed her like Consuelo? I have proof you killed her, you know."

At once Cindi knew she had made a mistake. She had pushed Cliff too far this time. The look of lust left his eyes and they now beamed with fury instead. His face lost all its appeal. His suave facade crumpled. His mustache twitched.

"You know too much. You little bitch, I'll shut you up," he vowed in a low, monotonous tone. He reached for Cindi, but she was too quick.

With a growl, Tai grabbed for Cliff's trousers. He hung on like a bulldog, hampering the man from going after Cindi.

Cindi dashed onto the brick patio only to be stopped short by the huge panther. In the light of day, the beast loomed twice as large as ever. Its dark fur gleamed with an oily sheen.

The long, prehensile tail made a hypnotizing motion, as measured as the ticks of a metronome. She shrank back against the wall of the pool house.

From within the pool house, she heard Tai whimper. Then he burst out the door running as if he'd never stop. Cindi remembered what Consuelo had written. Instead of following the dog, she stayed put.

Indeed Consuelo's words seemed true. She really had nothing to fear for all the animal's attention was centered on Cliff who had followed her out onto the patio once Tai loosed him. He was intent on silencing Cindi, but the beast caused him to change his mind.

The panther refused to allow Cliff to get near her, moving closer and closer to Cliff with inexorable intent. Cliff began to run for the woods. The cat bounded after him in an easy lope. Cindi swooned. Her head took most of the impact from the brick patio.

*　　*　　*

After a stop at Rives Style Shop on the way to Shreveport, Dell kept glancing at his reflection in the mirror of the truck. He tried to keep his eyes dutifully on the road, but every chance look in the mirror showed an unfamiliar reflection. He hardly recognized the man he saw. Most of his shoulder-length hair lay on the floor of Rives Style Shop. He shook his head. Even the weight of his head seemed all wrong, the color of his hair darker as well.

He figured in time he'd get used to the hair cut. He looked older and more mature, and that was good. Now perhaps Cindi will take him more seriously. Tucked away behind one ear was a single long strand of hair he'd refused to have cut. After the barber finished with the rest of his hair, he'd braided it. It would be an unobtrusive reminder. He shook the braid down, letting it hang loose.

A pile of paintings wrapped in brown paper was stacked on the seat beside him. A pair of brown loafers sat on top of them. Dell was prepared to put the shoes on, but not till he had to.

His secret destination was the Left Bank Art Gallery in Bossier City, Shreveport's twin city just across the Red River. Days ago, the manager, Mr. Delacroix, called to tell him they wanted to exhibit his work. The man suggested Dell bring more paintings for the one-man show they were planning.

Dell had wrapped and loaded everything he hadn't already sent to the gallery. He'd left Cindi's portrait on the easel, covered with his paint-daubed drop-cloth. He didn't want her to see it before he had a chance to explain how he happened to be inspired to paint it.

He breathed deeply, trying to calm his nerves. So much depended on this meeting. Until he and Mr. Delacroix shook hands on the deal, he would be unable to believe his good fortune. He wished he could talk to Mr. Jim.

CHAPTER 16

"You're sure no one's called with a message for me? My name is Dell Comeaux. You remember that old TV crooner Perry Como? You say my name the same way as his, but you spell it C-o-m-e-a-u-x," he repeated, slowly sounding out each letter of his surname to the girl at the rent-a-car desk. He was afraid someone else had taken the message before she came on duty, and because of the spelling the girl didn't know how to pronounce his unusual name.

Cindi was late. She was very late. As the girl at the counter shook her head to signify no messages, Dell felt his heart turn over, skip a beat and threaten to skid to a stop. He imagined Cindi taking a wrong turn and ending up in Texarkana or God knows where. He imagined Cliff or Samantha coming by and delaying her departure from the house. He imagined the panther hemming her up somewhere. He tried calling Magnolia House with no results except to hear his own recorded message on the answering machine.

Dell gritted his teeth to keep from swearing into the receiver. Instead in a controlled voice he intoned his message. "Cindi, where are you, babe? Please call me. I'm at the airport at the car rental counter." Dell left the number of the rent-a-car agency at the end of his message.

His high spirits over the sale of one of his paintings and up-coming show deflated as he realized selling his art meant nothing now that he couldn't find Cindi. Even having it on display was useless to him if anything had happened to Cindi. Without her, why did he care? He didn't give a damn if anyone ever bought anything he painted. But he had to have some means to support Cindi before he asked her to marry him. He looked on this show as the start to his paying career as an artist.

A cashier's check for the painting already sold rested in his wallet. The size of it proved he could support both of them by selling his art. A small velvet jeweler's box was in the breast pocket of his jacket. He planned to place these love tokens before Cindi during their celebration dinner at Monjuni's.

That's when he planned to ask her to marry him. Where was she? Where was his *querida*, his love?

Dell waited at the airport for almost an hour. An hour that seemed days long, as he paced or sat restlessly in the airport's uncomfortable, rigid plastic chairs. At any moment he expected to see Cindi dash through the doors, her long, pale hair swinging, her apologies for being late bubbling from her lips.

His images of Cindi only added to his restlessness. Like a movie, vignettes of her ran through his mind. Cindi standing in front of Magnolia House the day she arrived. Cindi on the quilt at St. Elisabeth's Baptist Church. Cindi in the pool in her seductive black swimsuit. Cindi basking in the sun on the patio in that teeny, hot pink bikini bottom. *What a babe. He just hoped she would want to be his babe. His wife.*

He'd waited as long as he could. He needed daylight for the drive home so he could see oncoming cars to check for Cindi. He left the airport, following the route they had discussed and agreed upon, but he didn't meet her.

"Dammit Cindi, you've got to be all right. You're the most important thing in my life, the only thing that matters," he hissed through clenched teeth. As the miles sped by, he became increasingly afraid for her. He pledged himself to cherish and protect her from now on. If only he got the chance.

An ominous pall in the direction of Magnolia House began to plague Dell as he neared home. Soon he could make out flames through the black haze. The smell of smoke seeped in through the air-conditioning vents of the truck. Was Magnolia House on fire? Somehow fire hadn't been among the catastrophes he'd imagined Cindi getting into.

"No! It's not Magnolia House!" He shouted the words in triumph as he passed Spoonful Bar. The ruined place was ablaze and disintegrating rapidly. What did he care? With renewed hope, he sped on.

At the exact time of day of Cindi's first arrival at the house, Dell pulled up in the driveway. It was moments after he'd left Spoonful Bar burning to the ground. Opening the garage door, he saw her car was still there. She'd never even left. Irrational anger rose, choking him. Suppose she'd just decided on a whim not to meet him.

He jumped from his truck and tore into the house shouting her name. Stillness greeted his calls. He yelled her name again. This time he was rewarded with the sound of Tai barking.

The barks held a note of alarm.

He dashed out to the rear deck. Then he saw her and his anger vanished as his hopes plummeted. She lay on her stomach, half in, half out of the shallow end of the pool. Her long blonde hair was matted with blood from a nasty looking gash over her left eye. Her head rested on the concrete edge of the pool. Tai stood protectively near, whining uneasily now that his barks had summoned help. Dell turned her over gently, and lifted her head.

"Ooh," she moaned. "My head hurts." She took a shallow, gasping breath.

"Come on, darlin'. Let's get you warm." He gathered he up, and headed for his own house. It was closer. She felt so cold. Her lips were blue, and shivers shook her frame. He realized she might be in shock.

"Who are you? Where's Dell? What are you doing here? You're not Dell. I want Dell," Cindi said, tossing her head back and forth on the futon where Dell laid her. He listened with dread as he dialed 911 for assistance.

"I need an ambulance fast. A woman has been injured. She has a head wound… No, I wasn't here when it happened, so I don't know how… Uh, just hurry. Oh yeah, down the main road there's a fire. It's the old Spoonful Bar. I guess you need to send a fire truck as well as an ambulance."

After giving the dispatcher directions again, he was finally able to turn back to Cindi. "Ssh, sweetheart," he soothed. "It's me, Dell. I'm here for you."

This time, since her eyes were closed, she allowed him to cuddle her close and help ease her chills by adding his own warmth to hers. He glanced up and saw his altered appearance mirrored in one of the windows and knew why she hadn't recognized him by sight. But she had known his voice.

Dell piled all the covers he had on her, and left Tai lying beside her to continue to warm her and watch over her. He went to the main house so he could guide the paramedics to the back. He hoped they would get here soon.

He had hardly formulated the thought, when he heard the wail of the siren. Lights flashing, the ambulance pulled to a stop before him. The emergency team jumped out.

"Follow me," Dell said, and led the way through the kitchen door, into the den and out the French doors. It was the closest route.

Cindi lay deathly still, as pale as the marble tile in Magnolia House's entry. Blood still oozed from the gash. While working on her, the paramedics questioned Dell, trying to discover how the accident had occurred.

"I found her this way," he admitted. "I went to Shreveport on business. She was supposed to meet me there. When she didn't show up, I came on back to see why."

"Were you worried about her?"

"Yeah, strange things have been happening around here. I was worried."

"Show me where you found her," one said.

"At the shallow end of the pool. She was wet and cold. She was semi-conscious then."

"I guess you had to move her, but with a head injury that's not the best thing to do," the paramedic said.

"Don't waste time jumping on me. Let's get her to the hospital."

The trip to St. Michael's Hospital in Texarkana seemed endless to Dell. The time he spent in the emergency waiting room as a team sewed up the wound and cared for Cindi was torment.

"You can see Miss Lynn now."

A green garbed nurse stood before Dell. He looked up, not realizing at first that she was speaking to him, not knowing who she meant.

"Miss Lynn?" He asked. "Oh, you mean I can see Cindi now?"

"Yes, Cindi Lynn."

"Please forgive me, I didn't recognize her by her last name."

"Are you close to her?" the nurse asked as she led him to Cindi's room.

"She's the most important person in my life."

"She's going to be fine in a day or two. But we'll have to keep her over night. Go on in, Mr. Comeaux."

Entering her room, he saw part of her beautiful hair had been shaved off. A large bandage covered the scalp wound. She looked so young, so pale, so drained. All the hospital equipment clustered around her bed intimidated Dell. He was glad her eyes were closed so she couldn't see the concerned expression on his face. By the time she roused enough to see him, he wore a more composed look.

"Hey babe, how are you feeling?" He asked, keeping his voice low and gentle. "I was so worried when you didn't show up. What happened?"

"I'm okay." But her words came out in a lifeless tone, though her voice was strong enough. "I went to your place looking for scissors. Cliff came. He looked at that picture you painted of me. Why did you do it?"

"Do it? What do you mean? I didn't do anything."

Cindi just stared at him. "Yes, you did," she said.

"Do you mean my hair? I had an interview. I wanted to look nice, civilized."

"Your hair? I didn't mean your hair. Why did you paint that horrible picture of me? You didn't tell me it was a nude painting. I look so big and ugly with no clothes on." Cindi looked anguished and distressed.

Dell hung his head. "I'm sorry you had to see it before I had a chance to tell you about it, *querida.* I don't think now is the time to talk about this. But I can explain. You look beautiful, and I thought if I painted you that way, you would always belong to me. No one would ever be able to take you away from me."

"Cliff saw it, too," Cindi said.

Dell felt raw jealousy pour over him. He'd ignored her the first time she mentioned Cliff. Now he knew that particular painting would never go on open display. "Cliff was there? It was never meant for anyone like him to see." Dell was so upset he wanted to slam the man with a powerful kick and finish him up with a karate side-of-the hand blow to the neck.

"Cliff saw it." Cindi said for the third time. "Oh Dell, how could you?"

"Please *querida*, I didn't mean to hurt you. The painting was meant to show my love for you, not for slime bags like Cliff Aymond to gawk at. It is a private thing for you and me alone, sweetheart."

But even though he spoke of love at last, Cindi turned away from him. She closed her eyes. Dell left.

*   *   *

Back at Magnolia House, Dell turned his hand to whatever job he could find. He needed to keep busy. But the house was spotless. He cleaned his own space till it was also.

He weeded the pink and white periwinkles in the front planters. The plants were in full bloom. He set the sprinkler to rotate on the front lawn, and water the grass and flowers. He wanted everything to look perfect when he brought Cindi home that afternoon. The night she spent away at the hospital had passed slowly for Dell.

The air was full of fragrances. The roses, the periwinkles, the dainty variegated blossoms covering the lantanas, which anchored the house at each end—each plant added its own distinctive fragrance. The magnolias had passed their prime. Instead of lemony blooms, they bore bright red seed pods. Dell gathered the ones that had fallen to the ground, putting them under the overhang of the garage to dry.

Barking came from the rear of the house. Tai had been barking and scratching at Cindi's patio door for hours. Now and then he raced around the side of the house and looked anxiously at Dell as if asking why Cindi wasn't opening the door for him. Finally Dell went and let the dog into the empty suite. There Tai whined uneasily, circled three times and then collapsed on the rug where he usually slept.

In the sudden, welcome silence, Dell heard the sound of a car on the drive. When he went to see who was there, he found Samantha Carver opening her car door.

"I thought I'd come by and pick up the books Cindi borrowed from the library."

"That's very nice. I'll get them. You know she fell yesterday and hurt her head." Dell told Samantha all he knew about Cindi's accident as they moved through the foyer and hall.

Samantha followed him into Cindi's room, listening intently.

"She'll be fine, Dell. She's young and strong. Don't worry about her. I think you must really care about her."

"Yes, ma'am, I do." As he used the word he often used as a joke with Cindi, he felt like crying.

Tai heard Samantha. He whined from the doorway and wagged his tail until she went over to pet him as he stood there.

"Tai's looking good, Dell. I'm glad I gave him to you. I know Cordelia would be glad, too."

Dell heard a new lucid tone in Samantha's voice. She was speaking as if she knew her daughter was gone. Tai had been Cordelia's dog once. Samantha had been unable to bear the sight of him after she died. Now here she was, petting the dog, acting as normal as anyone. He didn't feel he should comment on that though.

"I'll be going to pick Cindi up in an hour or so. Why don't you stop back by to see her on your way home?"

"I'd like to, but I can't. I'm transferring back to the Shreveport library. That's where I'm headed now. That's why I came by for the books. I wanted everything to be in order when I left this branch."

"Transferring to Shreveport." Dell shook his head in wonder. "I thought you didn't like the commute."

"I won't be commuting. I'm leaving Jeff because he stays high on drugs. I'm taking back my life. I'm starting therapy. I think in time I'll be fine. I know now that Cordelia's gone, and denying it won't change a thing. Wish Cindi luck for me."

Samantha left him wondering and speechless. He went back outside to finish his yard work and ponder what she'd said. Deputy Morgan pulled into the driveway thirty minutes later as Dell raked leaves and debris.

"Just wanted you to know Jeff Carver has been arrested for distribution of controlled substances and bringing in illegal aliens. I think the charge will stick. Heads are going to roll in the sheriff's department as well."

"What about Cliff Aymond? Has he been questioned yet?"

"We won't be able to question him. His partially burned body was found in the old bar down the road."

"You mean Cliff's dead?" Dell couldn't believe it, couldn't imagine why the man had been anywhere near Spoonful Bar. "Wonder what he was doing there."

"Well, I'm not sure," Morgan said. "You'd think no one would want to torch such an old structure, but it looks like arson. And not a very expert job of arson at that. Some inflammable substances were found near Mr. Aymond's remains. I don't suppose you've heard from Rita Gomez, have you? We really need to question her."

"I don't know if anyone will ever be able to question Rita," Dell said. "I'm not sure she's still alive. While I was in Cindi's hospital room, she kept muttering that Cliff had killed Rita like he did Consuelo Flowers."

"Looks like I need to speak to Miss Lynn then. You say she's in the hospital?"

"Yes, she was hurt in an accident late yesterday. She'll be home this afternoon. I think she'd be glad to talk to you."

"That's good," Morgan said. "You know it's odd about old Spoonful. We found a recent addition at the rear of the bar. Kind of a lean-to affair. It wasn't visible from the road. I don't know when it was added. It was partially burned as well, but we could tell it was used as a kind of bunk house. Probably to house those people they were bringing in. We found some of them there as well—twelve very frightened, very grateful to see the fire truck Colombians."

"What is going to happen to the South Americans?" Dell asked.

"They might have to go back, but there are certain hardship scenarios where they might be allowed to stay."

"Cliff Aymond was here the day Cindi had her accident. The day of the fire."

"Now I know that I'll be back later to see Miss Lynn."

* * *

Cindi twisted in pain on her hospital bed. Her skull was sore, as was her right shoulder. Her feelings were raw and sore, too. She didn't know what she would say to Dell when he came to pick her up. Still angry and upset, she was afraid she'd say the wrong thing. Unable to stay on the bed, she got up and went to the mirror. She loosened the clamp holding her hair up, and nervously twisted her long tresses around. It didn't help, even with her abundance of hair; she couldn't cover where her tresses had been shaved. With the bandage covering her injury, she looked pathetic, and there was no way to disguise that either.

"I look like a forlorn, little twerp again," she muttered. "Just like when I was twelve years old." She sighed and wondered again what she would say to Dell. She wondered why he hadn't told her about the painting. She wondered why she hadn't sensed even in her sleep he was there watching her as she sunbathed in her bikini bottom. There was no other time he could have seen her that way. That probably meant he started the painting before they'd been intimate the first time.

A persistent honking sounded outside. She went to the window to look out. In the parking lot below, she saw Dell's pickup. Tai was in the back wagging his tail off and barking. Dell waved from the open window.

A nurse pushing a wheel chair entered. "Looks like your family is glad you're going home," she said. "Are you happy? You don't look it."

Cindi tried to smile. She wished Dell and Tai were her family. If they weren't, she had none, since her father might never be found. Her father might even be truly dead.

No, she decided. She had no real family. And she had no real home either.

"I don't have any claim on those two," she told the nurse. "If I want one I have to make a claim."

Dell entered in time to hear her cryptic last words. "Ready babe?" He asked.

"Yeah, let's get out of here."

The whole ride home, Cindi sat without saying much. Dell made quips that fell flat. He told her all the news. About Samantha and what Deputy Morgan told him about Jeff Carver. Cindi expressed gladness over Samantha's return to mental health. When he told her about Spoonful and Cliff's death, she didn't say anything for a while.

Just before they reached Ida, she talked about what happened to her.

"I'm just glad Cliff won't have a chance to be the governor of Louisiana," she said finally. She grew even quieter then. After a mile or so, she said, "I wonder how he got to Spoonful. The panther chased him away from the pool house."

"I pulled the covering off the easel and saw my picture. I thought Tai and I were alone. I told the dog how I felt about it. Cliff scared me when he spoke. I looked at him and his face had a dreadful, leering expression. I hated him seeing the picture. He came towards me. He said my painting was beautiful."

"I never meant him to see it," Dell said. He glanced at her and saw she looked miserable. "Sorry, babe. I've already told you that. I'm sorry he was there, too. I'm glad he got what was coming to him, too. I hope to be forgiven for saying it, but I'm glad."

"Maybe he did get what he deserved. I asked him about Rita. I asked if he killed her the way he did Consuelo. He didn't answer, but he tried to grab me. Tai stopped him by latching onto his leg and holding on for dear life."

"Did Cliff hurt you?"

"No, I ran out onto the patio thinking I could get away, but the panther was there."

"The panther? Dear God, no wonder you were in shock when I got home."

Cindi shook her head. "I wasn't afraid of the panther. I was afraid of Cliff. Consuelo told me not to be afraid of the panther." *Or Cordelia.* She told Dell about the letter she'd found from Consuelo. Most of it. "That's how I can be sure Cliff killed her. And the panther, Delia, protected me when Cliff got away from Tai and came out on the patio to get me. He chased Cliff away. I guess I fainted and fell down. I hit my head, but I think I saw them running for the woods."

"Morgan is coming over to ask you some questions when we get home. You've got lots to tell him."

"I wonder if he'll believe me."

"How did you get in the pool?" Dell asked.

"You won't believe me."

"Try me," Dell answered.

Cindi told him about the insubstantial wraith of a girl who had helped her up from the pool house patio. A girl she imagined was Cordelia with dark hair and the same lost look she'd seen in Samantha Carver's eyes. A girl who helped her down the path to the main house, but whose strength had begun to wane as they neared the pool. Then Cindi fell and the girl wasn't able to keep her from falling. The effort she made to help caused her form to waver and disappear.

"I fell into the water. Cordelia was gone, but Tai pulled me out. You know how he hates the water, but he helped me until I could rest my head on the edge. He stayed right by me. Every time I came to, I saw him there watching over me."

"You saw Cordelia," Dell said.

"I truly believe I did. Consuelo told me not to fear the panther or Cordelia's ghost either. She must have known the girl's spirit was still around here."

Dell didn't answer. Cindi petted Tai, and crooned nonsense to him, calling him her brave lion dog and praising him for saving her. Tai wagged his tail and made a happy sound of his own.

Dell wished he felt as close to Cindi as Tai apparently did.

Hearing about Cordelia had shaken him, but he knew Cindi was the woman he loved. She had allowed him only one small kiss and only the slightest embrace before they left the hospital. He knew he had to ask her to forgive him. For painting her nude without her permission, for failing to be there when she was in danger. He wondered if she would forgive him. If she could forgive him.

"Do you still want to know about my appointment?" He asked.

"I'm not consumed with curiosity anymore, but yes, I would like to know why you wouldn't tell me."

"I was afraid to tell you. Afraid it wouldn't work out. I saw the man who runs an art gallery in Bossier City. He's been examining some of my paintings. I'll be having a one-man show there next week."

For the first time since their ride began, Cindi smiled. "That's great, Dell," she said. "I'm so happy for you."

She even looked happy. Dell took heart.

"There's more. He's already sold one of my paintings. He gave me the check for it that day. I was planning to put it in your hand when we had dinner that night."

"In my hand?"

"Yes. Right after I placed this on your third finger, left hand."

By now they were back at Magnolia House, though still in the truck. Dell pulled out the jeweler's box. "Cindi, please forgive me. And if you can forgive me, and you still love me, will you marry me?" He held out the open ring box.

Cindi didn't answer. She didn't take the box. She just looked stunned. As Dell tried to pull her into his arms, she resisted.

"I'm not saying I will marry you, but I'm not saying I won't," she said. "I have to have time to think about this. Until then, I can't take your ring."

"I did it all for you, Cindi. I wanted you to know I could support you before I asked you to marry me. The show's not really for me. Being successful isn't important to me. Being famous either. I don't even care about having that much money. But I do need you."

"I just can't say yes right now, Dell."

"Fine," he answered, but he didn't sound as if he meant it. "If that's the way you feel, I don't think I can stay here. Tai can stay to protect you."

"You don't have to do that, Dell. Can't you stay at the pool house like before?"

"After what we've been to each other?"

He looked so sad Cindi wanted to relent, and give him some encouragement. She wished she could, but caution kept her silent.

She went into his arms then, and embraced him. Being in his arms made her feel she was truly home again. She felt safe and warm. The warmth grew as he kissed her face, pressing kisses on each eyelid, moving to her cheeks and ear lobes until Cindi knew she must respond more. She pressed closer to Dell, but as she did, he moved away as he had done once before.

"I want you to come to me with your whole heart, Cindi," he said. "If you think you will be okay here with Tai, I'm going on back to the gallery. I'll stay in town for a while."

He moved to get out of the truck. They heard a vehicle coming up the drive.

"Must be Deputy Morgan," Dell said.

But as Cindi and Dell moved to the garage doorway, a taxi drew up. A tall, thin man with a white crew-cut stepped out and reached over to pay the driver who was taking out his bags.

Cindi couldn't believe her eyes. "Father," she cried.

CHAPTER 17

"Father, is it really you?" Cindi asked. Tears of joy streaming down her face, she ran to him. Throwing her arms around him, she hugged him tightly.

"Cindi, you're still here. You're all grown up," was all Jim Lynn could manage to say as he hugged her back. "I was hoping you'd stay."

"I'm so glad you're here, Father." She stood back looking at him. "You're alive. Cliff told me you were dead."

"Ah, my partner, Cliff, a scoundrel and a half," her father said. "I knew he would be trying to convince you I was dead."

"Come sit on the porch, Father. I think there are tales you have to hear. Many things we have to tell you. And some of them aren't very pleasant," said Cindi. "Come, and you can tell us how you got here. The last thing Cliff told me about you was that you'd been killed trying to escape. I'm so glad he was wrong." Cindi held on to her father's arm, only letting go when they found seats in the rockers there.

Dell watched the reunion as he held Tai securely. The dog pulled mightily, straining to get away and attack the man who might hurt this woman he would protect with his life. He growled and began to bark. Cindi noticed Tai's distress. The wrinkled canine gave a mighty tug and managed to break free. He lumbered over and stopped short when he realized Cindi was in no danger.

"Yes, it's all right," Cindi said, to the dog whining at her feet. "Tai, this is my father, Mr. Jim." Tai scooted over to Jim Lynn's feet, whining and wanting to make amends. His stubby tail wagged furiously.

"Where did this outrageous animal come from?" Jim asked. "I don't remember him."

"Samantha Carver gave him to me. He was Cordelia's dog," Dell explained.

Cordelia's dog? Cindi was struck dumb at this information. Over the roaring in her ears she heard her father ask, "Are things so dangerous we need a guard dog around Magnolia House now?"

"You're just joking, Father, but strange things have been going on here." She looked at Dell, a silent appeal in her eyes.

"What is it Cindi?" Her father asked. "What has been happening? Why is your head bandaged? Where is Cliff Aymond? Most of all I want to know where Consuelo is. I need to know." Now his eyes held a silent appeal.

"Your partner, Cliff Aymond is dead," Dell said. "And I'm afraid before he died, he murdered Miss Flowers. I'm sorry , Mr. Jim."

Jim Lynn stared at Dell. His face grim and ashen, he suddenly looked much older. "Not Consuelo, not my brave sweetheart. I knew something was wrong when she never came to help me." He got up from the rocker and began to pace the length of the small porch. "I hoped against hope she was still alive, but I knew something was wrong all along."

"She's gone, Father." Cindi said. "I'm sorry, too. I've been wishing ever since we found out that I could have known her. I'm truly sorry you've lost her." Cindi stood up and threw her arms around her father again. "Let's go on inside. We can hear your story there."

They entered the house. Tai refused to follow. Once inside, they turned in one accord away from the formal rooms to head for the den. When they were settled there, Jim Lynn asked once more what had been happening and why Cindi's head was bandaged.

"Tai and Dell saved my life yesterday."

"What happened? Is that why you look like the walking wounded?"

"You got it." Cindi laughed.

The sound of her free-hearted joy tugged at Dell's heart. "Tai and I didn't do it all. The panther had something to do with it, too," he said.

"The panther. As in Delia, the legendary monster of Loggy Branch?" Lynn asked. "This is a tale I've got to hear."

The story came out first in Dell's words, then Cindi's, but neither told of the painting Dell had done of her.

"All that really matters is that I'm fine. Cordelia and Delia helped me, but Tai and Dell saved me. I don't look fine, but my scalp will heal, my hair will grow back," Cindi finished.

"Now it's time to hear what happened to you, Mr. Jim," Dell said, as he moved closer to Cindi and took her hand.

"You know, and I guess Cindi does, too," Lynn began, "that I went to Colombia over two years ago to design and oversee the building of a house like this one. It was to be for Raul Gomez, Consuelo's uncle. When the house was almost finished, the police arrested Gomez. He was executed. Primarily for smuggling emeralds, as well as people, and narcotics. And he was holding out on the government, he wasn't giving the police their piece of the action.

"The police took possession of the house. Rita, his daughter, and I moved into a smaller place. I was asked to design a house for one of the government officials. In return, I would be paid with my safety and a meager stipend. I began to work on another set of blue prints. Rita stayed with me. She had no family left and nowhere to go. She insisted on doing the housekeeping and cooking for me."

"I knew it!" Cindi exclaimed. "I thought she was Consuelo's cousin. And I wondered why she was working for you when she acted as if she wasn't used to being hired help. As if she'd been born to better things."

Jim Lynn smiled, a weak smile, but still there. "Rita was good help, but you're right. She thinks she should be the one being served, not the server. She had a jealous heart, and a mean streak as well. She always begrudged Consuelo everything she had." He paused and took a deep breath. "I still can't believe Consuelo is gone." He covered his eyes.

Cindi gave his hand a sympathetic pat. "I'm so sorry, Father," she said.

Dell left for the kitchen. In the silence before Jim began to speak again, they could hear the sounds of water running, then the sound of dripping coffee.

Jim lifted his head and smiled again. "Strong Colombian coffee, the cure for all ailments—even heartache."

"That's right," Dell said, returning with a tray of cups and a carafe of the wonderful brew.

After a few sips, Jim was ready to continue. "Back to Rita. She expected to come to America with me when my job was through. To live here at Magnolia House with Consuelo and me. I should have left Colombia right then, but I didn't. I shouldn't have tried to finish the job. Then I wouldn't have been arrested. Rita wouldn't have had to leave the country. Maybe Consuelo wouldn't be dead."

Cindi jumped in at that. The things she said were meant for Dell, too. She hoped he knew that. "You know you can't blame yourself for Consuelo's death. We always can see what we should have done when the time for action is past. All of us do that, but we can't let 'what if's' and 'I should have's' keep us in an emotional stew. You're home now, and I'm glad. Did you really ask Rita to tell me to stay here at Magnolia House?"

Cindi's headlong speech, and her quick-change question made her father smile—more broadly this time. That was the result she was hoping for.

"Yes, I told Rita to ask you to stay. She came to see me in prison and told me she was leaving Colombia on one of the smuggler's flights," her father said. "Consuelo got word to me that your mother had died. So many deaths," Lynn stopped and shook his head, but he didn't stop long. "Consuelo told me she was asking you to stay here while she worked on getting me out of prison. I hoped you would find peace here. I hoped you would want to stay on once I got home. I'm still hoping you will. Now that Consuelo is gone, the house will belong to me. We had made our wills—necessity in this state, the only state in the union whose laws are still based on the Napoleonic Code."

Cindi felt Dell's gaze, and wanted to flash him a tiny smile, but instead she just said softly, "Maybe I will stay on at Magnolia House."

"So how did you finally get to the States?" Dell asked then. He was hoping Cindi would stay, hoping she would accept his ring. Cindi's soft words had given him those hopes.

"I faked my own death. I was being moved to another prison by plane, a sea plane. The guards thought they had killed me when I made my escape. But I eluded them, and made my way to a friend who got me on a steamer bound for New Orleans."

"So all along Cliff was feeding us some of the truth," Cindi said. She began to tell how Cliff had kept her in turmoil, claiming first that her father was alive, then dead. "I suppose his news was coming in with the smuggled goods and people."

Once again, she didn't mention the nude painting or how Cliff surprised her when she found it. She wanted to keep her father from knowing of her quarrel with Dell, who she could tell was fidgety and uneasy.

Dell listened to what she said and what she left out. He realized she was going to need time away from him to come to her decision. But he wanted Mr. Jim to know how he felt about his daughter even though she seemed unwilling to say anything about their relationship. He supposed he would have to make good his plans to leave Magnolia House.

He stood and said, "It's time I started for Bossier now. I need to be close to the gallery to help get the paintings ready for the show."

This remark brought on a new round of explanations so that Jim Lynn could learn of Dell's good fortune. After the explanations were done, Cindi walked with him to the garage. They stood near his old truck. He held her tightly, desperately.

"Babe," he told her, "all you have to do is call me if you want me back. You know what I want from you. I want you to promise to be my wife. When you know what you want from me, call me."

Cindi, very near tears again, sighed and said, "I just can't say I will marry you. When I know the answer to that, I'll call you." She kissed him goodbye. "Father and I will see you at the gallery on opening night. We'll be there."

* * *

Cindi stirred uneasily in her sleep. She reached for Dell, but he wasn't with her in the big bed in the master suite. She still slept there. Her father had refused to move her out of the rooms she had occupied since she arrived at Magnolia House. He would not want to sleep there without Consuelo anyway. He had taken one of the pristine second floor bedrooms Cindi had worked so hard cleaning.

The stealthy sound came again. Cindi woke enough to know she had sent Dell away. He wasn't even in the pool house. He had rented an apartment in Bossier. He'd been there for days now. Ever since her father returned. She ached for him, and knew in her heart she had wronged him.

A quiet rustling among the tropical trees and bushes in the atrium grew louder and louder. The moon was in the first quarter, a puny thing that gave little help. Cindi blessed the light from the bathroom, which she now let burn every night. Her last encounter with the panther had left her wary and skittish.

A sibilant whisper pierced the darkness. "*Senorita?* Miss Cindi?"

Cindi sat bolt upright in the bed. "Rita? Is that you? Are you a ghost or flesh and blood?"

"It is me, Rita, solid flesh and blood. I came to bring back the pianos I take and these cursed emeralds. I have had nothing but bad luck since I take them."

Cindi turned on the lamp beside her bed. A bedraggled Rita, hair escaping from its usual braids, stood before her. "What happened to you?" Cindi asked.

"Don't ask. I've been staying in the storage shed at Carver's airstrip ever since I leave here. Well, not quite the whole time. At first I was with Cliff, but I get so mad at him, I decide I go home to Colombia, so I go to Jeff's to wait for a helicopter to take me home."

"And there won't be any more helicopters leaving from Carver's air strip. Jeff's been arrested for smuggling dope and people in from Colombia."

"I wonder what happen. I don't see Jeff or Cliff for days now. I don't see anybody. Today I eat the last of the supplies I bring with me when I left and I drink all the coffee."

"Cliff is dead, Rita."

"*Madre dios,* Cliff is dead. When did this happen?" Rita's shrill voice rose in a shriek. "Even when he treat me like dirt, I still care for him. He promise me he will help me get home. Now I know why he never come." She broke into noisy sobs.

"Rita Gomez, I'd know that voice anywhere," Jim said from the doorway.

Rita let another shriek. "Mr. Jim, you are alive. That make me so happy. Sad—happy, happy—sad, I do not know how I feel."

Cindi invited her father in. She reached for her robe. "We might as well be comfortable. Let's go sit in the sitting room. I think Rita has lots to tell us."

"Yes, you are right. I have to tell you how I take the emeralds and two of Consuelo's little pianos and leave Magnolia House. I think when I leave I will soon be back. That is what Cliff said. So I take nothing else with me except the clothes I am wearing and my sleeping togs."

"How did you find the emeralds? Why did you only take two of the pianos? How did you decide which ones you wanted?" Cindi's barrage of questions poured out all at once without a pause for answers.

Her father laughed. "Come on, Cindi. Give Rita a chance to answer you. Slow down a little bit."

"Thank you, Mr. Jim. Cindi, I think you know I snoop around your rooms all the time. I find all the hiding places here. I know my cousin Consuelo so well, I find where you put the emeralds in her desk without too much trouble. The little pianos belong to me first. I just took them back. One of them is a laser. It will throw a picture."

"Wait a minute," Jim Lynn said. "Didn't you get money from

Consuelo when you *sold* her those trinkets? And what do you mean throw a picture?"

"Yes, Consuelo pay me for them, but she is dead. Why shouldn't I take them back?" Rita defended herself by asking a question of her own.

"How did you know Consuelo is dead? Did you have a hand in her murder?" Cindi asked.

"No, I would never kill my cousin," Rita denied. "Cliff kill her before I even got to Louisiana. He came here because he thought he could use the house to keep some of the people here. The ones who came in from Colombia. He need more room, because there were supposed to be more people on the 'copter I was coming on. Consuelo say no. She want you to stay here. She told him she was going to Colombia to get you out of prison, Mr. Jim."

Jim had been toying with the miniature pianos. "Ah," he said in a satisfied voice as a wavering three dimensional image appeared in the chair nearest the fireplace.

The ghostly illusion strengthened, and Cindi once again saw the specter she'd been calling Cordelia. Even when she knew it was a trick, the sight brought chills to her spine.

"It was all a trick?" She asked. "The ghosts, the piano and everything?"

Rita shrugged. "Not all of it, *senorita*. The night we see *el tigre* was no trick. I did not do that. I do not make the voices or the panther. The only trick was the image of the girl the piano would throw."

"But that's what I saw that first night right?"

"*Si*, you see this," she gestured to the holograph. "You hear recording of Consuelo playing the piano. Cliff wanted me to scare you so you would leave."

"But in the letter I found, Consuelo named you as her murderer, Rita," Cindi said.

"No, I would not do that. I am sorry Cliff killed her. I think he did not mean to. At least that is what he tell me." Rita's eyes shone with intensity as she attempted to convince Cindi and Mr. Jim of her innocence.

"Okay, I believe you," Jim Lynn said.

"Where did you go when you left?" Cindi asked, wanting to know if she and Dell were right about the footprints they'd found.

Rita told of her nightmare trip through the woods to Jeff's helicopter place. She told them she was certain the Loggy branch

Monster had followed her through the woods.

"I think it is Consuelo become *el tigre*. But it is Delia, the Loggy Branch monster. She stalk me."

She told them of meeting Cliff, of going with him to Shreveport. She told how he brought her back to Jeff's to wait for transportation home to Colombia.

"But then he never came back, I decide to come here. If I brought back the things I took, Cindi will forgive me."

Rita wanted to stay.

"I work and clean for you. I have nowhere to go. I will never be first lady of Louisiana now," she ended on a fatalistic note.

"I've just finished cleaning the place to the nth degree. There won't be much cleaning to do for a while. But you can stay. Your room is empty. Really empty. I boxed up your clothes and put them in the storage room."

"Please stay. You can fix all my favorite foods," Jim Lynn said.

"Yes, Rita. I've tried to learn to cook those things. I'm improving, but I'm nowhere as good a cook as you are," Cindi added.

* * *

Cindi hardly recognized the handsome man in the tuxedo. The one who was accepting plaudits and compliments from one and all. The one who raised his head to scan and search the crowd time and again. Finally their eyes met in a heart-stopping glance that excluded the crowded room full of beautifully dressed people and the glorious paintings hanging everywhere. Excluded the noise of the crowd, the tinkling of laughter and champagne glasses.

Nothing and no one else existed for Dell and Cindi as they moved toward each other. Dell could see her answer in her eyes. He had seen it from across the room. He smiled as he took her in his arms.

"Hello, Dell," Cindi said, recovering from his embrace and torrid kiss. "Congratulations, you're a success."

"Not yet. Don't congratulate me yet. I need one thing to make my success complete. You know what that is. How about it, babe? What's the answer?"

Cindi tried to act demure and shy, but she couldn't carry it off. Tears welled up as she said, "You mean you'll still have me? You still really want me? If you do, the answer is yes."

"Yes! The answer is yes!" Dell's excited shout raised glances all over the room. Everyone saw him grab Cindi and swing her around in a circle.

"Mr. Jim," he shouted again. "We need to get ready for a wedding at Magnolia House."

EPILOGUE

Jamie Marie and Jacob toddled down the slope on the southern side of Magnolia House. Their childish treble cries carried back to Cindi and Dell as they watched from the deck. The children stopped to examine each new flower and stone they found. Cindi reached for Dell's hand. The heavy scent of the magnolias in full bloom once again filled the air.

The eighteen-month-old twins were the delight of their parents' hearts. And of their grandfather's who stood nearby. To Jim Lynn, they offered a new chance to nurture his own, and find forgiveness for past failures.

Tai lay near the twins. He'd transferred his guardianship to them.

Magnolia House was restful and quiet. The panther roamed no more. Cordelia had found rest. The beautiful summer morning held out its glories to Cindi and Dell and their family.

LYN LAWRENCE

With six children, seven grandchildren and three great-grandchildren, what should an old gray granny do? Bake cookies? Babysit? Maybe. Not many would begin a writing career that encompasses publication of a true crime and two romantic suspense novels plus several other manuscripts finished and in various stages of being finished, but Evelyn "Lyn" Morgan did.

Lyn Morgan, writing as Lyn Lawrence and Lawrence King, has plans to be the Grandma Moses of the writing world and of the screen writing world and perhaps even the song writing world. She could be because she also has two completed scripts with one in pre-production stage now. Her two scripts, written with a writing partner named Deborah McMartin, also feature three of her original songs.

Her first book, *Magnolia House*, has garnered many four and five star reviews. In September of 2001, *Stone Justice*, a true crime co-authored with Deborah McMartin, was released both as an e-book and in trade paperback. In December of 2001, *For The Weekend* was released in e-book form. Two romantic suspense novels and one true crime manuscripts had become available as books during the year of 2001. Morgan says she could be on her way to fulfilling her dreams.

Lyn still has time for her children and grandchildren. Her family, scattered across the 50 states, keep her busy traveling to visit them and they often appear back at the old homestead for visits. She loves to travel for research and writer's conferences as well.

Could be she's found the perfect way to spend her retirement.

24140227R00097

Made in the USA
San Bernardino, CA
14 September 2015